Barbara & Karl Kesel	Writers
Rob Liefeld	Penciller
Karl Kesel	Inker
Janice Chiang	Letterer
Glenn Whitmore	Colorist
Introduction by	Barbara and Karl Kesel

DC Comics, 1325 Avenue of the Americas, New York, NY 10019
A division of Warner Bros. — A Time Warner Entertainment Company
Printed in Canada. First Printing.
ISBN #1-56389-120-4
Cover illustration by Rob Liefeld & Karl Kesel
Color art by Glenn Whitmore
Publication design by Dale Crain

INTRODUCTION

Creation stories — how something came to be — are interesting animals. Look at the creation myths from the various cultures around the world. There's an eerie similarity between many of them, yet each is slightly different. It's almost as if there was one, true, core event that happened, and each interpretation pushed it in a different direction.

I'm sure the same can be said about Hawk and Dove.

This is my version of their creation story.

I broke into the industry as an inker — but always knew I wanted to write comics, too. I was probably pretty annoying about it. I proposed a new series to Karen Berger within my first three months in the business, John Byrne nicknamed me "The Kibitzer," and I overwhelmed John Ostrander with long letters about ideas for SUICIDE SQUAD. In the middle of all this — and more important than any of it — I became romantically involved with a shy young editor named Barbara Randall. I was inking the figure of the dead Dove on George Perez's "Crisis" spread in The History of the DC Universe, not crying tears over the death of the guy since he was pretty much a minor hero, but regretting the end of a really interesting team. I always liked Hawk and Dove. I always thought how they'd say "Hawk!" and "Dove!" and transform was really cool. Then it hit me: The mysterious voice that gave Hawk and Dove their powers could easily give the Dove powers to someone else! Maybe... a woman! I called Barbara as soon as I could. She sparked off the idea instantly and before even *we* knew it, we were co-writers.

Barbara took the idea to another new DC editor: Mike Carlin. He gave us a chance, was very supportive, and made us work damn hard. By the time of the 1988 San Diego Comics Con, we had an approved mini-series.

I met Rob Liefeld for the first time at that convention. Barbara introduced us. Rob's energy and enthusiasm was (and still is) infectious. His samples were very good. We thought he'd be perfect for the book.

Mike agreed — although it meant a miniseries about a pair of obscure heroes scripted by a young writer and her untried collaborator, and pencilled by a virtual unknown. Only the inker had anything close to a track record, and fans aren't known for buying books based on the inking.

The fans bought this book — and not because of the inking. I like to think they bought it because, as rough and

R.L.
K.K.

awkward as it is from time to time, there's an undeniable *life* to it... a real love of comics that we all poured into it.

Hawk & Dove trivia:

1. Barbara created Kestrel. Rob Liefeld designed the costume. Mike Carlin decided it would be purple — midway between Hawk's red and Dove's blue. It honestly never occurred to us that "Kestrel" was so similar to "Kesel," although every fan seemed to notice.

2. Rob insisted that we modify the original costume and let Dove's hair show. It was a very good idea.

3. Barbara Randall became Barbara Kesel between the inking of issues #1 and #2 of the miniseries. That's why the inking gets better.

4. Mike Carlin's one worry about the new Hawk and Dove was that if either one died, the voice(s) could easily replace them. This isn't good in comics. It led Barbara to create the star-crossed lovers M'Shulla and T'Charr and, eventually, to a pivotal story in the HAWK & DOVE monthly series establishing Hawk and Dove as the last of their line.

And then Dove was killed and Hawk became a murderous villain.

The end.

Well, maybe not. See, now that I'm writing a monthly series for DC again, it's crossed my mind that the second Dove's death was very different from the first's, and it's just possible that...

Of course, if enough fans want it, *anything* is possible.

Karl Kesel
7/7/93

Here's how I remember it:

Back when I was newer to comics, I met this really nice guy. I have pictures of him I drew when I was in college. I met him three years after I graduated. He had all these sketchbooks I'd pore over while I waited for him to finish his quota of work for the day. One day I ran across a sketch of Hawk & Dove. Him and...her?

I was immediately excited about the idea. I burst up from my chair (in my usual sanguine fashion) and excitedly asked Karl where she had first appeared... when had they decided that Dove should be female? Of course! It was so obvious! The perfect partnership...yin and yang! Brains and brawn! Rage and patience! Blah, blah, blah! (Of course, you have to imagine the delivery at 78 RPM...)

"Oh," said Karl, "*That*. I never liked Dove as a guy. Too wussy. I always thought Dove should be a girl."

That's how it started.

At the time, I was posted in the zoo office next door to Carlin. We had originally pitched Hawk & Dove as a feature for an anthology book Carlin was developing, but Mike saw the potential and developed it as its own miniseries instead. I knew Rob's work from several sets of samples he'd sent to the office, and I knew he'd be right for the book (with Karl's inking, of course—the necessary topper to any artist we brought in on the project—no bias here, Sarge), so I pestered Carlin unmercifully until he agreed to add a complete unknown to an underpedigreed project.

And then it sold out. Cool.

This book was always very personal. It has its roots in real people: Karl's sister and my brother were the original models for the characters of Dawn and Hank (but only the good parts!); our parents became their parents; our friends became their friends. Kestrel's name was an inside joke: my friend Ron had used the name (it's a bird, look it up) as a gaming character—the most peaceful and loving character in the history of role-playing—so we used the name for our vicious mass murderer. Ren started out as my best friend, but just wouldn't stay her. As writers, we're always cannibalizing from our own lives in order to create *true* false reality, and there is, therefore, a lot of us in the mix.

This series always was about, if anything, love: the way it can invade and change your life without any respect for the way things had been, or perhaps *should* have been... Our love, and the feeling that a complementary partner is important to our own completion. Love for others, and what it will let you give up or give of yourself...

The book always was, and always will be, my favorite wedding present. I hope you all enjoy opening our gift.

Love,
Barbara (and Karl!)
7/7/93

HAWK
&
DOVE

DC
HAWK & DOVE™
FIVE ISSUE MINI-SERIES
BY KESEL, LIEFELD & KESEL
GHOSTS AND DEMONS!

JACKIE CHAMBERS, IS IT? THESE PICTURES--YOUR FAMILY? PRETTY WOMAN--WIFE? DAUGHTER? I'D LIKE TO MEET HER. HAVEN'T CHANGED YOUR CURRENCY YET, I SEE. SLOPPY...
FIRST TIME IN NICARAGUA, JACKIE?

I'M LOOKING FOR SOMEONE WHO WAS IN NICARAGUA NOT LONG AGO. MAY STILL BE HERE. AMERICAN MALE.
A LOT LIKE YOU, JACKIE...

HE LOOKS SO NORMAL, JUST LIKE ANYBODY. BUT JUST SAY THE MAGIC WORD AND HE BECOMES VERY STRONG. VERY TOUGH. VERY DEADLY.
A LOT LIKE ME.

I'M EVERYTHING HE IS, AND MORE. THE MASTERS SAW TO THAT. M'SHULLA AND GORUM. EVER HEAR OF THEM, JACKIE?

I GUESS THEY'RE WHAT YOU'D CALL GODS OF EVIL. THEY'RE LORDS OF CHAOS, JACKIE. I WORSHIP THEM.

MY NAME IS KESTREL.

I'M TO FIND THIS MAN. SPEAK TO HIM. JUST TALK. THAT'S ALL. HONEST.

BUT IF HE DOESN'T WANT TO LISTEN TO ME... WELL, MY MASTER GAVE ME--
--AN EDGE...

SKREEEECH

HOT KNIFE AND BUTTER. KNOW WHAT I MEAN?
STEEL. BRICK. BONE.
ALL THE SAME TO ME.

NOW WE KNOW MY NAME. AND WE KNOW YOUR NAME. BUT WHAT'S THE NAME OF THE MAN I'M LOOKING FOR?
CAN YOU HELP ME, JACKIE? DO YOU KNOW HIS NAME?

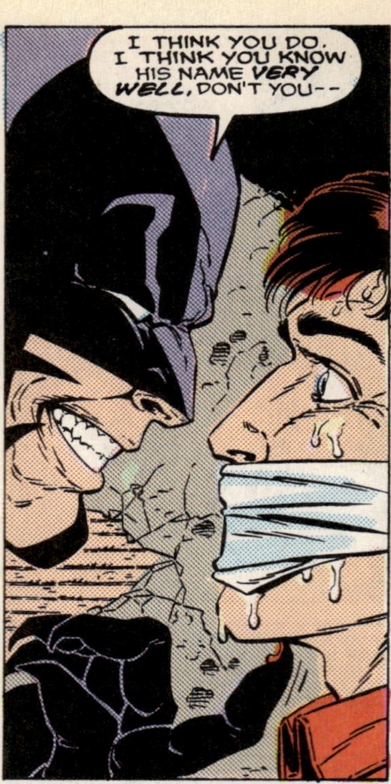
I THINK YOU DO. I THINK YOU KNOW HIS NAME VERY WELL, DON'T YOU--

HAWK!
SNIP

NO! NO! YOU GOT THE WRONG GUY! I'M NOT HIM! I'M NOT HAWK!

I'M NOT HAW--
I KNOW. I BELIEVE YOU. YOU'RE NOT HAWK...

...JUST LIKE ALL THE OTHERS...

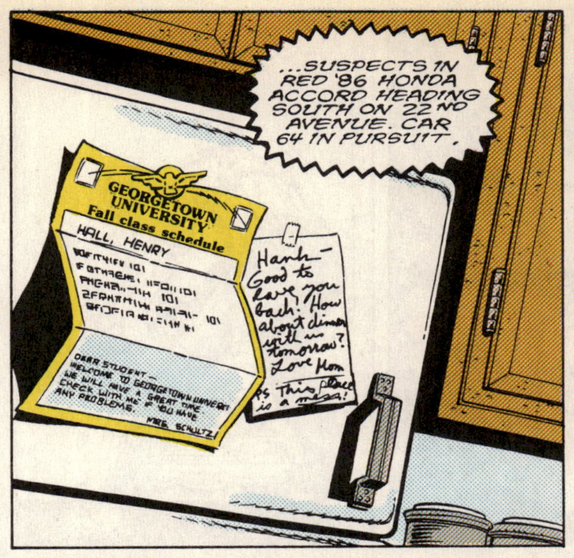
...SUSPECTS IN RED '86 HONDA ACCORD HEADING SOUTH ON 22ND AVENUE. CAR 64 IN PURSUIT.
GEORGETOWN UNIVERSITY
Fall class schedule
HALL, HENRY
DEAR STUDENT— WELCOME TO GEORGETOWN UNIVERSITY. WE WILL HAVE A GREAT TIME. CHECK WITH ME IF YOU HAVE ANY PROBLEMS.
MRS. SCHULTZ
Hank— Good to have you back! How about dinner with us tomorrow? Love Mom
PS This place is a mess!

CAR 64, THIS IS CAR 37-- SUSPECTS JUST TURNED WEST ONTO "M" STREET.
"M" STREET'S UNDER CONSTRUCTION-- THEY'RE BOXED IN. THEY'LL HAVE TO HEAD OUT AT WISCONSIN.
GUNS & AMMO
HEAD 'EM OFF--IF THEY MAKE IT, THEY'LL HAVE A CLEAR SHOT AT THE BRIDGE AND THE STATE LINE.

WE'VE GOT THE BACK DOOR, 64. YOU SWING AHEAD AND CUT THEM OFF AT THE PASS.
SEPT 10 5:12 PM
WILL DO, COWBOY.

CAR 37--THIS IS 64. WE'RE STUCK IN RUSH HOUR HERE. REQUEST BACK-UP.
HOLY--! THIS IS 37... THEY'RE SHOOTING AT US AND...
MIKE!
OH, GOD, THEY'VE HIT MORAGHAN, MIKE! MI--

37? YOU THERE? OVER.
ALL FREE UNITS, CONVERGE ON WISCONSIN AND M STREETS. SUSPECTS IN RED '86 HONDA ACCORD. ARMED AND DANGEROUS. ALL UNITS--

DAMN! IF NOBODY STOPS THEM THERE, THEY'RE HOME FREE!

WISCONSIN STREET
UNGHH!
C'MON...
...C'MON!
CATCH THIS--LOOKS LIKE SOME STUPID KID'S TRYING TO PLAY HERO!
HE BETTER--THIS CAR AIN'T STOPPIN' FOR NO KID!
DON'T LOOK LIKE HE'S GONNA MOVE.
HAWK.
OH, NO! NOT HIM!
GET OUT OF HIS WAY! GET OUT OF HIS WAY!

HAWK™ & DOVE
GHOSTS and DEMONS
KARL KESEL & BARBARA KESEL WRITERS • ROB LIEFELD PENCILLER • KARL KESEL INKER • JANICE CHIANG LETTERER • GLENN WHITMORE COLORIST
RENEE WITTERSTAETTER - ASSISTANT EDITOR • MIKE CARLIN - EDITOR

STREET
M STREET
KERASSH!
COME ON OUT, BOYS! YOU'RE MY FIRST CUSTOMERS, SO YOU WIN THE PRIZE!
UHFFF!
YOU'RE LUCKY I CAN AFFORD TO KILL YOU, YOU CRAZY--
NO WAY THE BOSS'D KNOW.
OOOWWW!
LUCKILY, I'M MY OWN BOSS!
PING
PING
BLAM
BLAM
I THINK I WINGED 'IM!
YOU TAKE THAT SIDE.

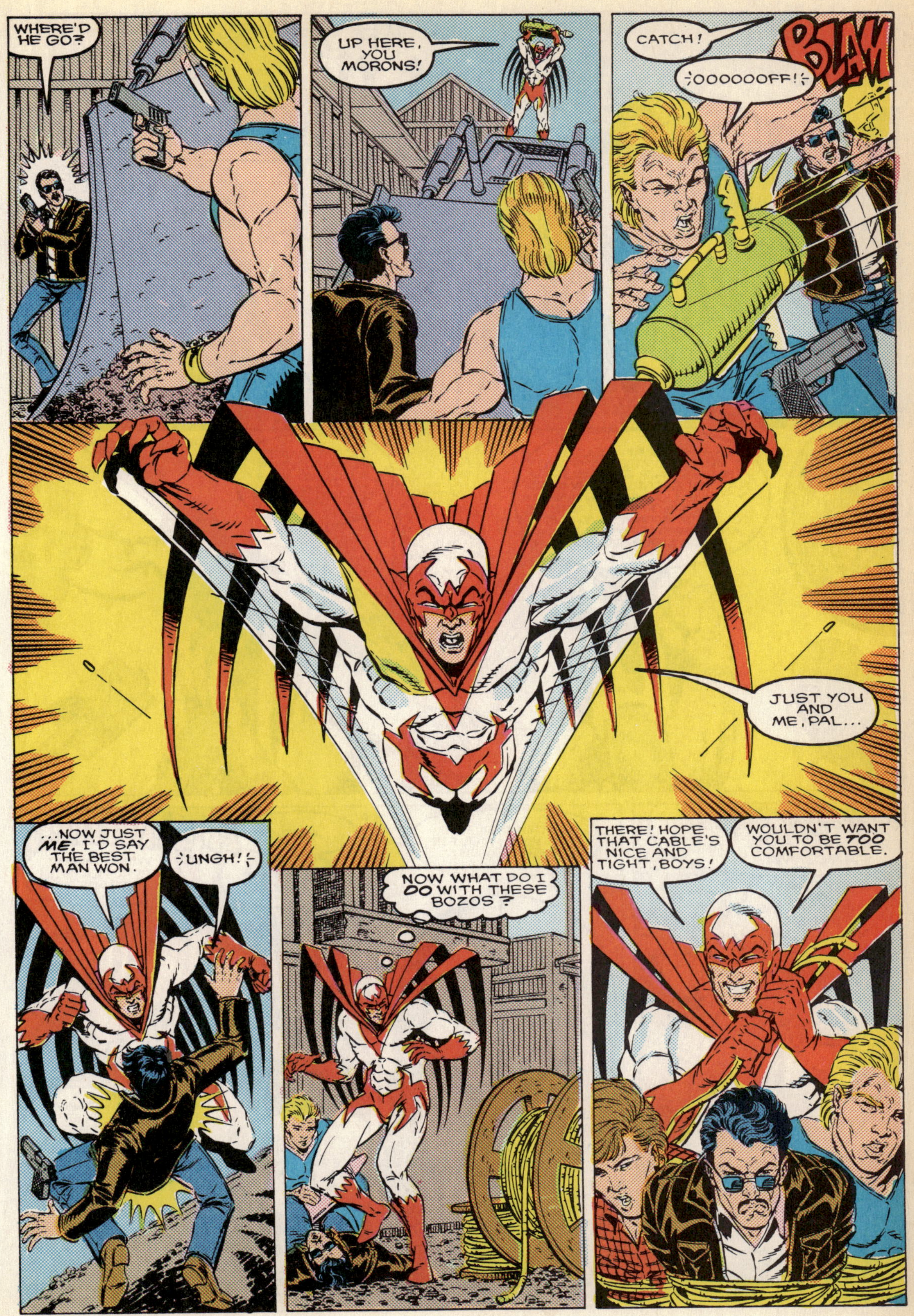
WHERE'D HE GO?
UP HERE, YOU MORONS!
CATCH!
BLAM
OOOOOOFF!
JUST YOU AND ME, PAL...
...NOW JUST ME. I'D SAY THE BEST MAN WON.
UNGH!
NOW WHAT DO I DO WITH THESE BOZOS?
THERE! HOPE THAT CABLE'S NICE AND TIGHT, BOYS!
WOULDN'T WANT YOU TO BE TOO COMFORTABLE.

I LOVE THIS JOB!
DON'T WORRY. EVERYTHING'S UNDER CONTROL, KIDS.

AS YOU CAN TELL, I'VE RESUMED MY STAY IN THIS FAIR CITY, OUR NATION'S CAPITAL, AND IF YOU'VE GOT ANY CROOKS LISTENING OUT THERE, TELL 'EM HAWK'S BACK AND THEIR DAYS IN D.C. ARE NUMBERED.
DOES THAT MEAN YOU'VE LEARNED HOW TO COUNT, HOTSHOT?

HELLO TO YOU, TOO, OFFI-- DETECTIVE WOLFSON! LOOKS LIKE YOU'VE GONE UP IN THE WORLD--AND AROUND!
VERY FUNNY, HAWK. WHERE'RE THE PERPS?

WADDLE RIGHT THIS WAY, WOLFIE, RIGHT OVER...
...HERE?

HAHAHAHA
I FEEL SAFER ALREADY.
THINK MAYBE METROPOLIS'LL TRADE?
YEAH, WITH HAWK AROUND, NO STEEL CABLES WILL DARE ROB ANY BANKS!
WANNA POSE WITH THE CROOKS, HAWK?

GET OUT OF MY FACE!
CRUNCH

HEY, MAN--
COOL IT, HAWK.

OKAY, WE'VE RECOVERED THE MONEY, THE LAB WILL GO OVER THE CAR AND WE'VE GOT THE FILM FROM THE BANK. ANY OTHER CLUES YOU MIGHT HAVE, HOTSHOT?
THAT'S HAWK. UH... NOPE.

THEN WE'LL JUST WHEEL YOU DOWN TO THE STATION FOR YOUR REPORT, AND--
UH, OH! THE DANGER MUST HAVE COMPLETELY PASSED--I'M CHANGING BACK!
LOVE TO, CHIEF, BUT I CAN'T. MEETINGS, Y'KNOW-- TITANS BUSINESS.

DETECTIVE...?
LET HIM GO. YOU WEREN'T AROUND THE LAST TIME HE SHOWED UP, BUT I CAN TELL YOU...

...WHEREVER THAT IDIOT GOES, TROUBLE IS SURE TO FOLLOW.
"TITANS' BUSINESS." HA! AS IF NOBODY KNOWS THE TEEN TITANS DUMPED HIM.

OH, MAN, IT'S ALMOST SIX!

I'M GOING TO BE LATE FOR...

"...FOOTBALL PRACTICE!"
CABOT! YOU CAN MOVE YOUR LEGS IN THIS GAME! IT'S ALLOWED! RUN SOMEWHERE OR PASS THE BALL! YOUR WING'S WIDE OPEN! PASS THE--

OOF!

CABOT, YOU MORON! WHY WON'T YOU LISTEN TO ME? YOU GOT NO EARS? YOU GOT NO EYES? LORD KNOWS YOU GOT NO--

AT LEAST HE'S ON THE TEAM, HALL.
COACH-- LISTEN TO ME-- WHAT'S WRONG WITH CABOT CAN'T BE FIXED! LET HIM JOIN THE PEACE CORPS-- GET HIM OUT OF THE COUNTRY! IF THERE'S EVER A WAR, I DON'T WANT HIM IN THE DRAFT POOL!

LUCKILY, I AM AVAILABLE. AND WITH ME ON THE TEAM, YOU COULD EASILY DUMP SULLIVAN AND BATRON, TOO. CLEAR OUT THE DEADWOOD.
EVERY DAY YOU COME DOWN HERE, HALL, AND EVERY DAY YOU ANNOY ME A LITTLE BIT MORE.

TRYOUTS WERE POSTED, AND YOU DIDN'T EVEN SHOW.
I DIDN'T EVEN KNOW I WAS IN COLLEGE! I WAS OUT OF THE COUNTRY, COACH! I WAS... UH... TIED UP!*
*LITERALLY, IN SUICIDE SQUAD/DOOM PATROL SPECIAL #1.

GET OFF THIS FIELD, HALL. YOU DISRUPT ANOTHER PRACTICE AND I'LL GET SECURITY AFTER YOU.
BUT--
GOOD-BYE, HALL!
TWEEEEEEET
OKAY, BOYS--TRY IT AGAIN. OH, AND CABOT--YOU CAN MOVE YOUR LEGS IN THIS GAME. IT IS ALLOWED.

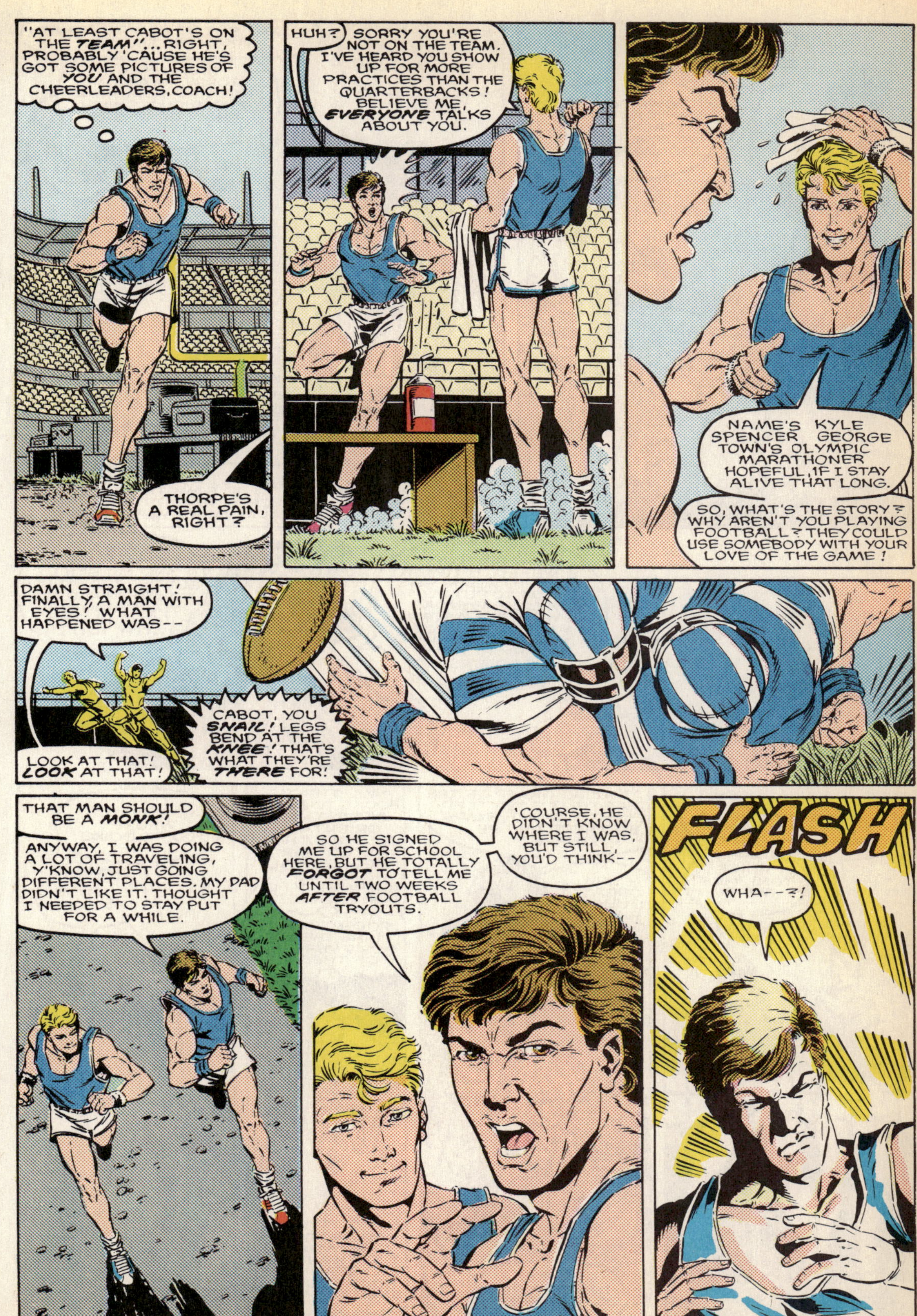
"AT LEAST CABOT'S ON THE TEAM"... RIGHT, PROBABLY 'CAUSE HE'S GOT SOME PICTURES OF YOU AND THE CHEERLEADERS, COACH!
THORPE'S A REAL PAIN, RIGHT?
HUH?
SORRY YOU'RE NOT ON THE TEAM. I'VE HEARD YOU SHOW UP FOR MORE PRACTICES THAN THE QUARTERBACKS! BELIEVE ME, EVERYONE TALKS ABOUT YOU.
NAME'S KYLE SPENCER GEORGE TOWN'S OLYMPIC MARATHONER HOPEFUL, IF I STAY ALIVE THAT LONG.
SO, WHAT'S THE STORY? WHY AREN'T YOU PLAYING FOOTBALL? THEY COULD USE SOMEBODY WITH YOUR LOVE OF THE GAME!
DAMN STRAIGHT! FINALLY, A MAN WITH EYES! WHAT HAPPENED WAS--
LOOK AT THAT! LOOK AT THAT!
CABOT, YOU SNAIL! LEGS BEND AT THE KNEE! THAT'S WHAT THEY'RE THERE FOR!
THAT MAN SHOULD BE A MONK!
ANYWAY, I WAS DOING A LOT OF TRAVELING, Y'KNOW, JUST GOING DIFFERENT PLACES. MY DAD DIDN'T LIKE IT. THOUGHT I NEEDED TO STAY PUT FOR A WHILE.
SO HE SIGNED ME UP FOR SCHOOL HERE, BUT HE TOTALLY FORGOT TO TELL ME UNTIL TWO WEEKS AFTER FOOTBALL TRYOUTS.
'COURSE, HE DIDN'T KNOW WHERE I WAS, BUT STILL, YOU'D THINK--
FLASH
WHA--?!

HEY! I'M GONNA--
DOWN, BOY! IT ISN'T AN ENEMY ATTACK--JUST MY GIRLFRIEND'S GONZO ROOMIE.

KYLE, I DIDN'T KNOW YOU HUNG OUT WITH SEAN PENN! MADONNA AROUND?
CLOSE, BUT NO KEWPIE. RENATA TAKAMORI, THIS IS--
HANK HALL. SORRY, MA'AM. I'VE JUST HAD SOME BAD EXPERIENCES WITH PHOTOGRAPHERS LATELY...
WELL, WE'LL JUST HAVE TO DO SOMETHING TO CHANGE YOUR OPINION, WON'T WE?

NOW BACK UP, BOYS--IT'S TIME TO GET TO BUSINESS. GOT TO PUT MY UNIQUE VISION TO WORK IF I'M GONNA MAKE FRONT PAGE NEWS OUT OF THIS SORRY BUNCH OF LOSERS!
KYLE--DONNA, YOU AND ME STILL GETTING TOGETHER TONIGHT? AND ARE YOU BRINGING SEAN HERE WITH YOU?

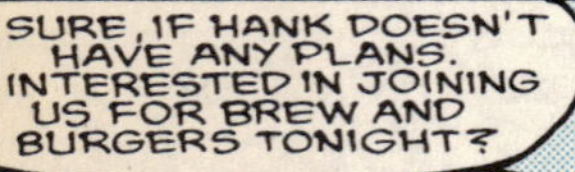

SURE, IF HANK DOESN'T HAVE ANY PLANS. INTERESTED IN JOINING US FOR BREW AND BURGERS TONIGHT?
HUH? TONIGHT? ME?

AMAZING GRASP OF THE FACTS! IT'S SETTLED. EIGHT TONIGHT. SUDS. BE THERE AND BE SQUARE!
SURE... GREAT! I GUESS I SHOULD GO SHOWER AND STUFF... UH, SEE YOU.
SEE YOU TONIGHT, REN. 'BYE! C'MON, HANK!

ALL THESE BOOKS TO BUY. "UNDERSTANDING ORIENTAL CULTURE," HUH. WHY BOTHER?... "GEOLOGICAL POLITICS"... "CHEMISTRY FOR NON-SCIENTISTS"...
DOESN'T SOUND LIKE THERE'RE MOVIE VERSIONS OF THESE...
WAITAMINNIT! CHEKHOV? THEY WANT ME TO READ A BOOK ABOUT STAR TREK?!

HEY! WATCH WHERE YOU'RE GOING!
EXCUSE ME, I--

LINDA! SORRY, I--
NO, HANK, I'M THE ONE WHO'S SORRY.
IT'S... BEEN A LONG TIME.
WELL, OUR PATHS DON'T EXACTLY CROSS ANY MORE.
NOT SINCE DON DIED.
Y'KNOW, HE WAS SO KIND AND CARING. THAT'S WHAT I LOVED ABOUT HIM. NOT THAT WE WERE GOING TO GET MARRIED OR ANYTHING, BUT...
FUNNY, I'VE NEVER MET TWO BROTHERS WHO WERE SO DIFFERENT. I ALWAYS THOUGHT THAT IT WOULD BE YOU--
YOU TWO WERE SUCH RIVALS, ALWAYS TRYING TO PROVE THE OTHER WRONG. IF ONLY YOU'D TRIED TO COOPERATE, MEET EACH OTHER HALFWAY...
...YOU BOTH COULD HAVE GAINED SO MUCH.
DON'T YOU MISS HIM?
I CRIED ALL THROUGH THE FUNERAL, BUT YOU WOULDN'T KNOW, WOULD YOU? YOU WEREN'T THERE. SOMETHING URGENT IN--WHERE?-- NEW YORK?
NO, LINDA, I--
SORRY, HANK. GOTTA RUN. YOU KNOW HOW IT IS.
BUT I HAD TO GO...IT WAS IMPORTANT! I--
I MISS HIM, TOO.
YOU DON'T KNOW WHAT IT WAS LIKE. DON WAS ALWAYS IN THINGS OVER HIS HEAD. I HAD TO GO ALONG TO PROTECT HIM...KEEP HIM SAFE.
SOME JOB I DID. DON'S DEAD.
DOVE'S DEAD.
AIEEEEEE!
HAWK!
GREAT! JUST WHAT I NEEDED! I HOPE IT'S DRUG PUSHERS. I HATE DRUG PUSHERS!

GIVE UP. TWO OF YOU AGAINST ME ISN'T A FAIR FIGHT--
--AND I WOULDN'T WANNA HAVE TO HURT YOU.
NOT TWO...

THREE.
SURE, AND MISTER INVISIBLE'S SNEAKING UP ON ME RIGHT NOW. I DON'T FALL FOR OLD TRICKS LIKE THAT... I'M A PRO.

KRAK

STUPID MOVE, HANK! NEVER GIVE SCUM A CHANCE TO GIVE UP. THAT'S SOMETHING DON WOULD DO. TALK TO THEM...
THERE'S DON NOW, IN THAT SILLY DOVE OUTFIT. PROB'LY BEING NICE.
...ONLY ONE THING THESE CREEPS UNDERSTAND...

THAT'S YOUR ANSWER TO EVERYTHING, ISN'T IT, HANK? PUNCH 'EM OUT, RIP IT OUT, TEAR IT DOWN...
YOU DON'T HAVE TO USE FORCE TO BE STRONG. THERE'S ALWAYS ANOTHER WAY! IT'S BETTER TO BUILD THAN TO DESTROY, RIGHT, DAD?

DON, HANK-- I'VE TOLD YOU A THOUSAND TIMES, EVERY TIME YOU MAKE SOMETHING YOU DESTROY SOMETHING ELSE.
YOU'RE BOTH RIGHT, BUT UNTIL YOU CAN SEE THAT, YOU'RE BOTH WRONG.

DAD... DON...
WE CAN TALK ABOUT THIS LATER, HANK. RIGHT NOW I HAVE TO SENTENCE A CONVICTED MOB BOSS NAMED DARGO...
DARGO? NO! WAIT! THIS ALL HAPPENED YEARS AGO! YOU GAVE HIM THE MAXIMUM SENTENCE SO, HE PUT A CONTRACT OUT ON YOU, DAD...
...THEN HIS GOONS CAME AFTER YOU...

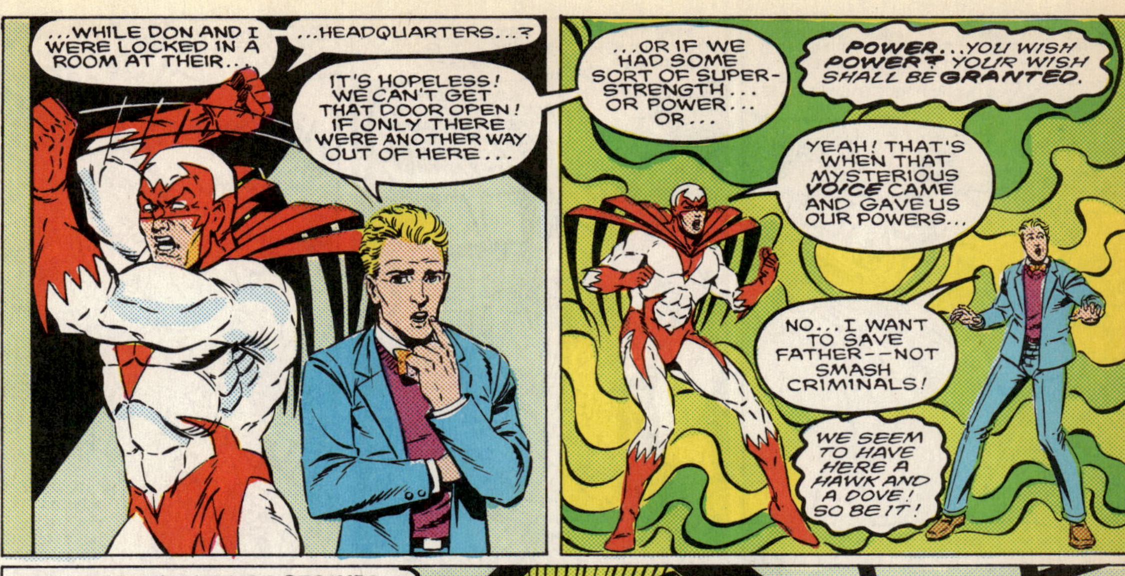
...WHILE DON AND I WERE LOCKED IN A ROOM AT THEIR...
...HEADQUARTERS...?
IT'S HOPELESS! WE CAN'T GET THAT DOOR OPEN! IF ONLY THERE WERE ANOTHER WAY OUT OF HERE...
...OR IF WE HAD SOME SORT OF SUPER-STRENGTH... OR POWER... OR...
POWER... YOU WISH POWER? YOUR WISH SHALL BE GRANTED.
YEAH! THAT'S WHEN THAT MYSTERIOUS VOICE CAME AND GAVE US OUR POWERS...
NO... I WANT TO SAVE FATHER--NOT SMASH CRIMINALS!
WE SEEM TO HAVE HERE A HAWK AND A DOVE! SO BE IT!

WHENEVER INJUSTICE STRIKES YOU NEED ONLY SPEAK YOUR NAMES--"HAWK" AND "DOVE"--AND YOU SHALL BE TRANSFORMED!
I KNOW! I KNOW! THESE POWERS WERE JUST WHAT WE NEEDED TO SAVE DAD...
WHATEVER YOU COULD DO MOMENTS AGO, NOW, IN COSTUME, YOU CAN DO INFINITELY BETTER YOU WILL BECOME EXTENSIONS OF YOUR INNER SELVES.
THE TRANSFORMATIONS WILL NOT OCCUR IF THERE IS NO INJUSTICE PRESENT, AND WHEN YOUR POWERS ARE NO LONGER NEEDED, YOU WILL REVERT TO YOUR ORDINARY SELVES...
WOW! THAT WAS A SNAP!

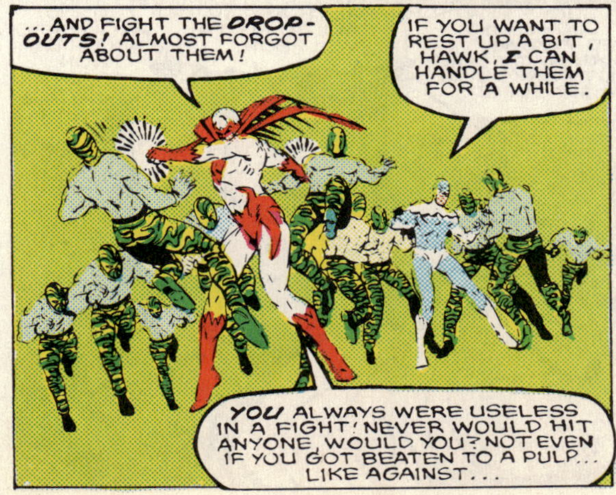
...AND FIGHT THE DROP-OUTS! ALMOST FORGOT ABOUT THEM!
IF YOU WANT TO REST UP A BIT, HAWK, I CAN HANDLE THEM FOR A WHILE.
YOU ALWAYS WERE USELESS IN A FIGHT! NEVER WOULD HIT ANYONE, WOULD YOU? NOT EVEN IF YOU GOT BEATEN TO A PULP... LIKE AGAINST...

...HARKER! TOUGH ESCAPED CON, BUT YOU WOULDN'T GIVE HIM THE ONE GOOD PUNCH NEEDED TO TAKE HIM OUT!
NO! I WON'T FIGHT YOUR WAY! I DON'T NEED TO USE BRUTE VIOLENCE ON ANYONE!
YOU FINALLY TIED HIM UP WITH HIS OWN SHIRT, BUT YOU LOOKED LIKE HAMBURGER FOR A WEEK! YOU JERK!

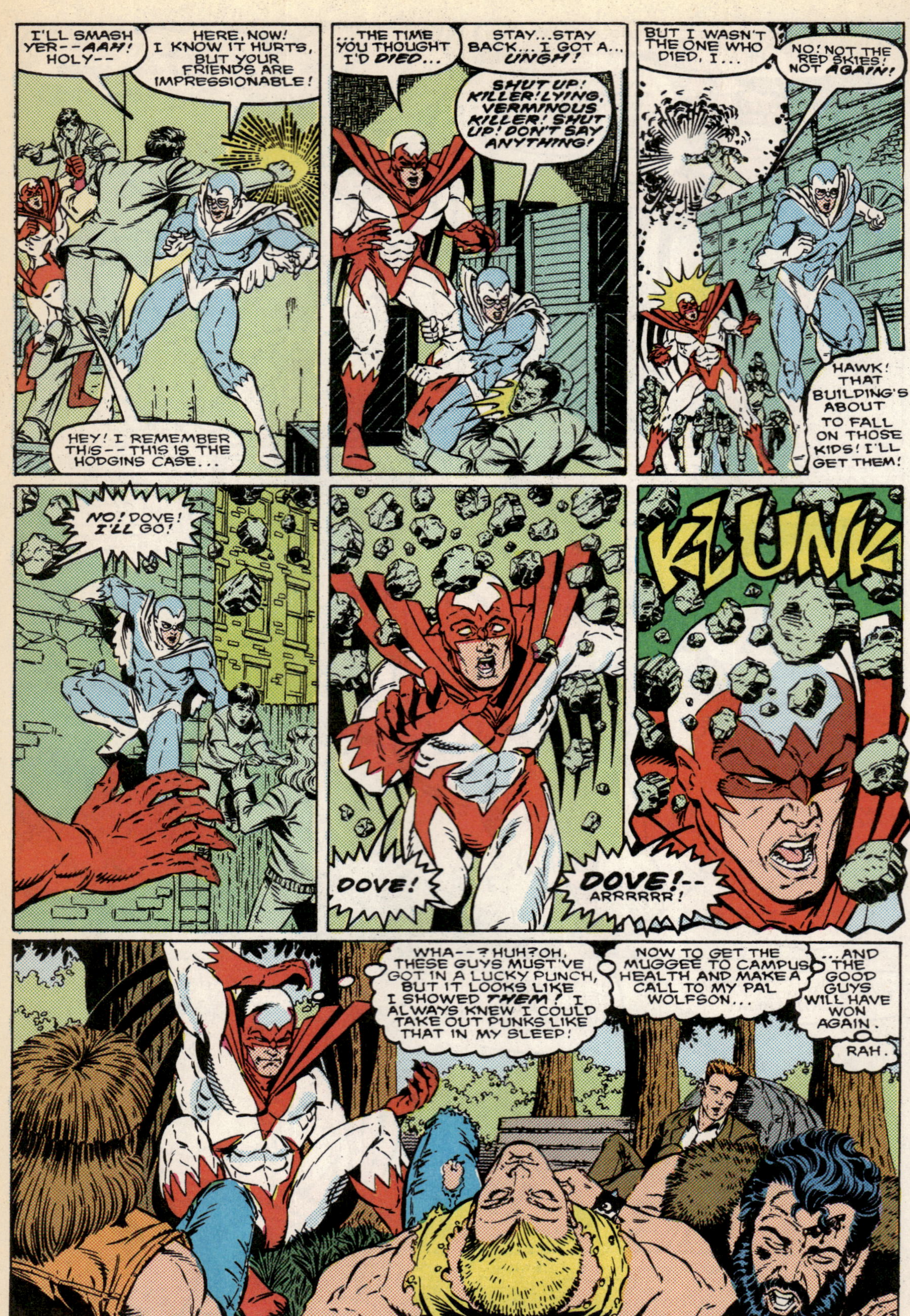
I'LL SMASH YER--AAH! HOLY--
HERE, NOW! I KNOW IT HURTS, BUT YOUR FRIENDS ARE IMPRESSIONABLE!
HEY! I REMEMBER THIS--THIS IS THE HODGINS CASE...
...THE TIME YOU THOUGHT I'D DIED...
STAY...STAY BACK...I GOT A... UNGH!
SHUT UP! KILLER! LYING, VERMINOUS KILLER! SHUT UP! DON'T SAY ANYTHING!
BUT I WASN'T THE ONE WHO DIED, I...
NO! NOT THE RED SKIES! NOT AGAIN!
HAWK! THAT BUILDING'S ABOUT TO FALL ON THOSE KIDS! I'LL GET THEM!
NO! DOVE! I'LL GO!
DOVE!
DOVE!-- ARRRRRR!
KLUNK
WHA--? HUH? OH, THESE GUYS MUST'VE GOT IN A LUCKY PUNCH, BUT IT LOOKS LIKE I SHOWED THEM! I ALWAYS KNEW I COULD TAKE OUT PUNKS LIKE THAT IN MY SLEEP!
NOW TO GET THE MUGGEE TO CAMPUS HEALTH AND MAKE A CALL TO MY PAL WOLFSON...
...AND THE GOOD GUYS WILL HAVE WON AGAIN.
RAH.

GATES 1-19
<TRANSAIR FLIGHT 203 FROM LOS ANGELES ARRIVING GATE 4.>
<AEROTOURIST PASSENGER JOHN GAUNT, PLEASE PICK UP WHITE COURTESY TELEPHONE.>

<MAY I HELP YOU, SIR?>
<YES, YOU CAN... EVA? IS THAT YOUR NAME?>
<WELL, EVA, I NEED TO FLY TO THE PLACE 2,100 MILES NORTHEAST OF HERE.>

<UH... DO YOU HAVE A SPECIFIC DESTINATION, SIR?>
<I THOUGHT YOU SAID YOU COULD HELP ME, EVA.>
<I WILL TRY, SIR.>
EVA

<MIAMI?>
<NO.>
<ATLANTA?>
<NO.>
<CHICAGO?>
NO!

<WASHINGTON, D.C.?>
<YES, WASHINGTON, D.C. ONE WAY.>

<THERE YOU ARE, SIR. EVERYTHING IS IN ORDER. YOUR FLIGHT IS BOARDING NOW, AT GATE 7.>
<GOOD. I HAVE TO ADMIT I DON'T LIKE WAITING, EVA. ESPECIALLY AT AIRPORTS. LATELY, TERRIBLE THINGS HAVE BEEN HAPPENING AT AIRPORTS.>

<IN THERE! A MAN! CUT! CUT INTO...!>
<CALL THE POLICE! SOMEONE CALL THE POLICE!>
<FLIGHT 313 TO WASHINGTON, D.C., NOW BOARDING AT GATE 7. WILL ALL PASSENGERS BOARD AT THIS TIME. FLIGHT 313-->

THIS IS STUPID! I'VE ONLY MET THESE PEOPLE *ONCE*...
SUDS

I'M NOT SURE I'D EVEN RECOGNIZE THEM...
YOU'RE HANK HALL, RIGHT? KYLE'S THIS WAY.
HUH?

HANK! GLAD YOU COULD MAKE IT! I SEE YOU FOUND MY GIRLFRIEND...
MORE LIKE ***SHE*** FOUND ***ME***. UH... HAVE WE MET BEFORE, MISS...

CABOT. DONNA CABOT.
CABOT?
BUT DROP THE "MISS" PART. IT'S JUST DONNA.
NO, WE HAVEN'T MET. I'VE JUST SEEN THE PICTURES REN TOOK OF YOU TWO TODAY.

AND SPEAK OF THE DEVIL...
HOWDY, PARDNERS! MR. CLOCK SAYS ONLY THREE MORE MINUTES UNTIL EIGHT, WHEN I CHANGE BACK INTO A NEARLY-NORMAL HUMAN BEING.
WELL, THEN, WISH NUMBER ONE: A LARGE PLATE OF FRIES...
JUST ENOUGH TIME TO MAKE YOUR WISH MY COMMAND!
WISH NUMBER TWO: A PITCHER OF SUDS' SPECIAL! HURRY, WENCH, BEFORE THE MAGIC FADES!
THEY LOVE THIS. IT'S THEIR ONLY CHANCE IN LIFE TO FEEL SUPERIOR.
AND THE USUAL ROUND OF CHICKEN BURGERS?
CHICKEN? DON'T YOU HAVE ***NORMAL*** BURGERS?
UGH! CAVEMAN NEEDS ***RED MEAT!*** WHY AM I NOT SURPRISED? SAYONARA, COWBOYS! BACK IN A FLASH!

MY ROOMIE. I GUESS I'LL KEEP HER.
WHAT'D YOU WIN?
I LOVE IT WHEN YOU'RE NOBLE.
BY THE WAY, HANK, WE'RE CELEBRATING MY WIN SATURDAY, SO TONIGHT'S ON ME. EAT HEARTY.
YOU PLAY TENNIS. HUH? ANY GOOD?
TENNIS MATCH.
BETTER THAN SOME, BUT I DON'T PLAY AS OFTEN AS I SHOULD.

BETTER THAN MOST IS WHAT THAT MEANS, HANK.
KYLE TELLS ME YOU LIKE FOOTBALL, HANK. I HAVE A BROTHER--
OH, GOOD-- JUST IN TIME! HERE COMES REN WITH OUR ORDER!

WITH EACH STEP OUR HEROINE COMES CLOSER TO ANOTHER FLAWLESS EVENING OF SERVITUDE WITH INFINITE GRACE--
OOPS!
OH, NO!

I BELIEVE THIS IS YOURS...

THAT WAS PRICELESS!
I'M SO SORRY! IT JUST HAPPENED SO FAST! POW! ZOOM! ARE YOU ALL RIGHT?
I'M FINE. REALLY, IT WAS MY FAULT. MY MIND'S ALWAYS FOUR STEPS AHEAD OF MY BODY.

I'LL JUST GET OUT OF YOUR WAY NOW, AND...
NOW, WAIT A MINUTE! AFTER AN INTRO LIKE THAT, WHY DON'T YOU JOIN US?
OH, I DON'T...
SIT.
WELL, OKAY.

YOUR VICTIM WAS REN TAKAMORI. THIS IS KYLE SPENCER.
I'M DONNA CABOT...
...AND I BELIEVE YOU'VE ALREADY MET HANK HALL...

CABOT... OF COURSE! I SAW YOU PLAY AT WIMBLEDON LAST YEAR! YOU DID VERY WELL, CONSIDERING THE GRASS COURTS. THEY'RE SO UNPREDICTABLE...
...AND DON'T YOU HAVE A BROTHER WHO'S...

HEY! DID YOU GUYS HEAR ABOUT THAT FIRST FEDERAL ROBBERY TODAY? HAPPENED RIGHT OUTSIDE MY APARTMENT, ALMOST... SO I GOT TO SEE HAWK IN ACTION!
I WENT OVER THERE LATER, AND LOOK WHAT I FOUND!

HOLY HOT LEADS, BATMAN! PAULSEN PHOTO-CHEMICAL-- THEY HAVE A WAREHOUSE ON THE RIVER.
REN, BE SERIOUS FOR A MINUTE... IF THIS HAS ANYTHING TO DO WITH THE ROBBERY, SHOULDN'T YOU TURN IT OVER TO THE POLICE, HANK?
COULD THEY BE HIRING EX-CONS OR--HEY, THIS WOULD BE WILD--WHAT IF THEIR LOW PRICES ARE SUBSIDIZED BY ILL-GOTTEN MEANS?

UH... YEAH! RIGHT! ALMOST WHAT I WAS THINKING! SORRY TO EAT AND RUN, BUT I JUST DON'T THINK THIS CAN WAIT!
'BYE.
WE UNDERSTAND.
BUT YOU'VE GOTTA COME BACK AND TELL US THE END OF THE STORY, OKAY?
UH... SURE. SEE YA TOMORROW. MAYBE.
I'LL BE HERE!

SUBTLE.
SORRY. SO I LIKE 'EM BIG AND STUPID. SO SUE ME.

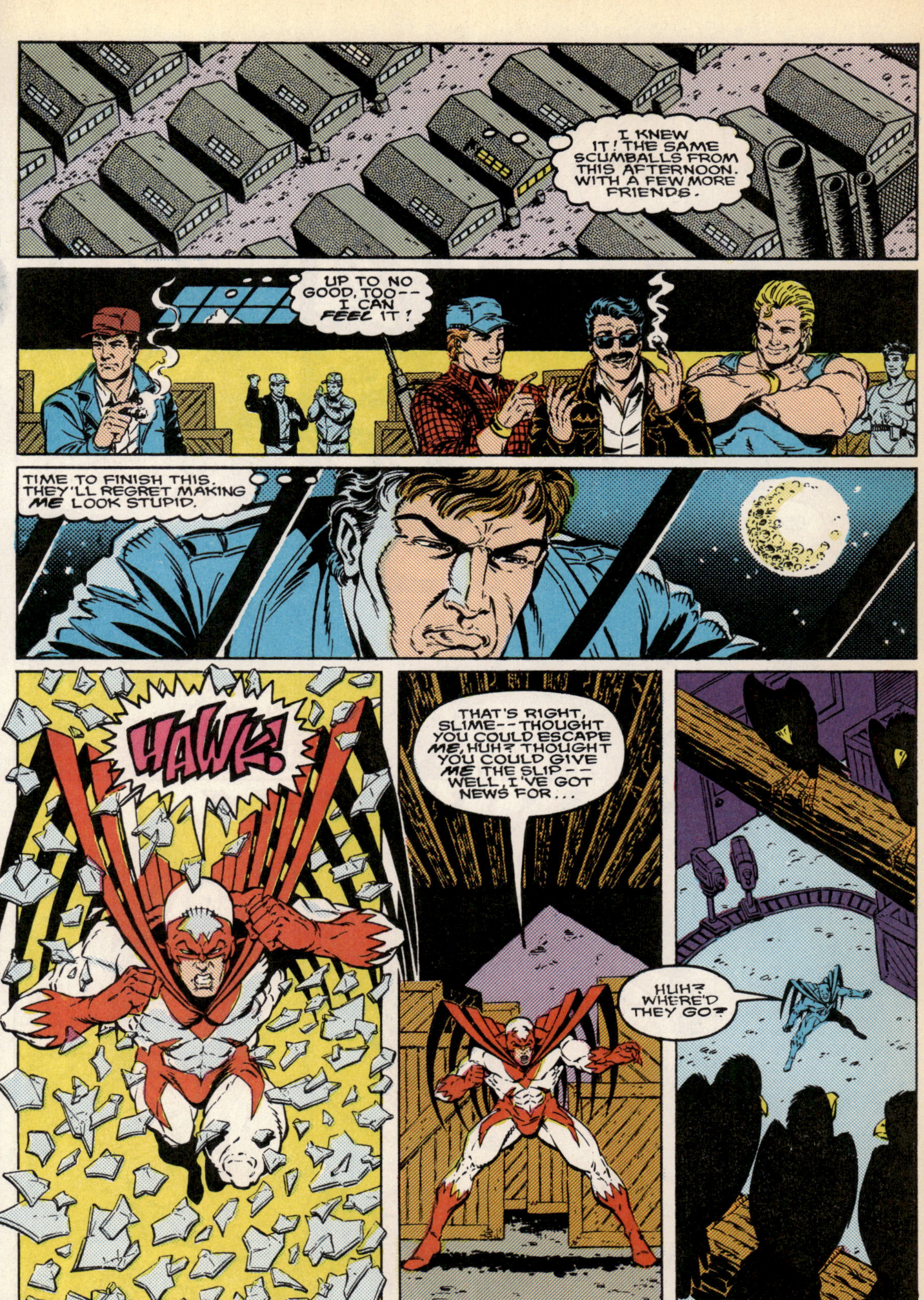
I KNEW IT! THE SAME SCUMBALLS FROM THIS AFTERNOON. WITH A FEW MORE FRIENDS.
UP TO NO GOOD, TOO-- I CAN FEEL IT!
TIME TO FINISH THIS. THEY'LL REGRET MAKING ME LOOK STUPID.
HAWK!
THAT'S RIGHT, SLIME--THOUGHT YOU COULD ESCAPE ME, HUH? THOUGHT YOU COULD GIVE ME THE SLIP-- WELL, I'VE GOT NEWS FOR...
HUH? WHERE'D THEY GO?

AW, COME OUT AND FIGHT LIKE MEN. WHY ARE YOU GUYS HIDING, ANYWAY?
AFRAID OF ME?

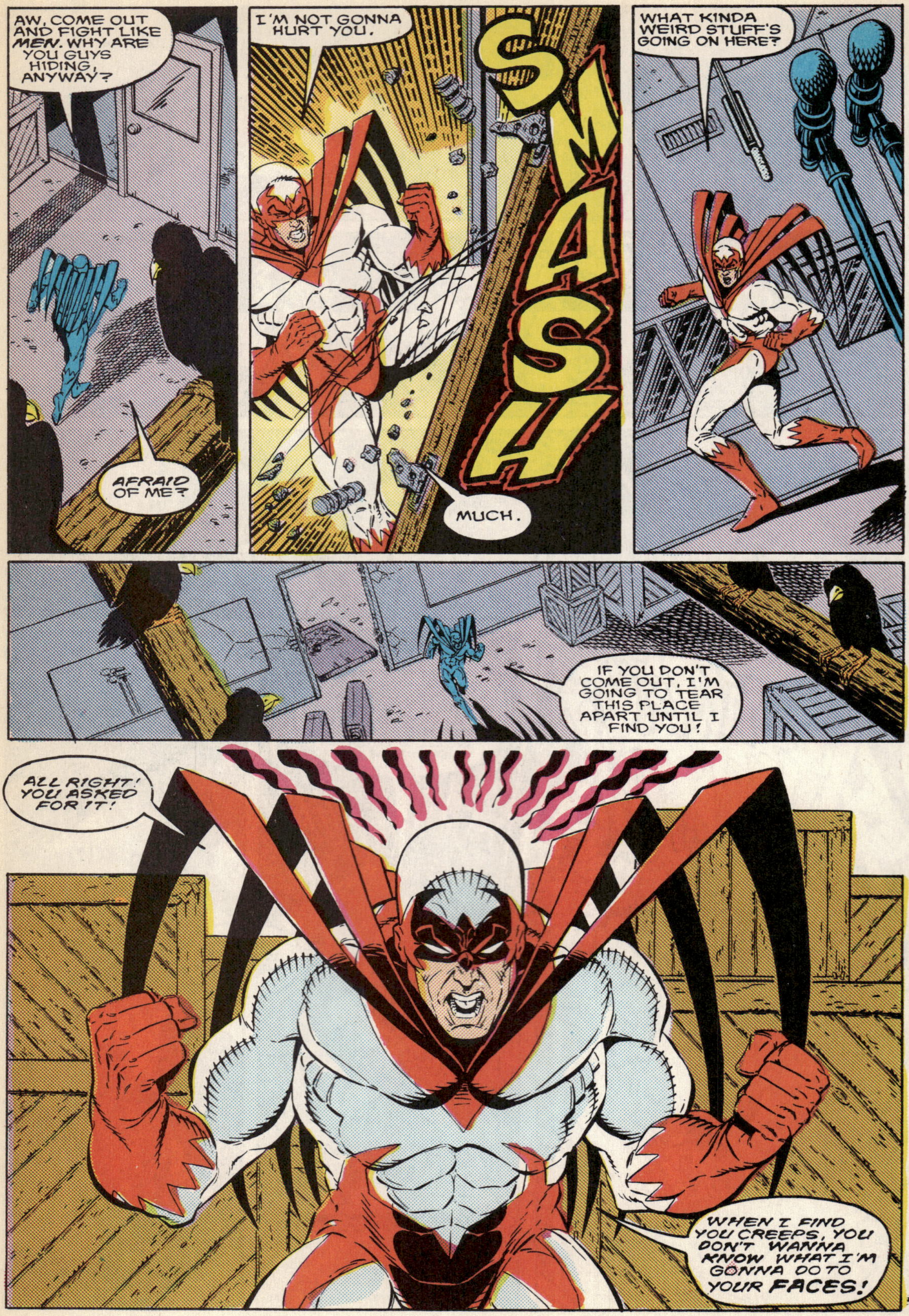

I'M NOT GONNA HURT YOU.
SMASH
MUCH.

WHAT KINDA WEIRD STUFF'S GOING ON HERE?

IF YOU DON'T COME OUT, I'M GOING TO TEAR THIS PLACE APART UNTIL I FIND YOU!

ALL RIGHT! YOU ASKED FOR IT!
WHEN I FIND YOU CREEPS, YOU DON'T WANNA KNOW WHAT I'M GONNA DO TO YOUR FACES!

CLICK
CLICK
CLACK
CLICK

IT'S ABOUT TIME!

DOES THE BOSS KNOW HE'S HERE?
YOU MIGHT AS WELL GIVE UP, HAWK. YOU'RE OUTNUMBERED.
IF HE DIDN'T, HE WILL NOW.

DON'T YOU GUYS READ THE PAPERS? THIS IS THE WAY I LIKE IT. JUST ME. JUST YOU POUNDED INTO GARBAGE.
I DON'T NEED A WEAPON, I DON'T NEED ANYBODY ELSE TO TAKE YOU OUT. I DON'T NEED--

DOVE.

TOGETHER AGAIN FOR THE FIRST TIME!

DC
HAWK & DOVE™
2
NOV 88
U.S. $1.00
CAN $1.35
APPROVED BY THE COMICS CODE AUTHORITY
FIVE ISSUE MINI-SERIES
BY KESEL, LIEFELD & KESEL
TOGETHER AGAIN FOR THE FIRST TIME!

HAWK & DOVE™
TOGETHER AGAIN FOR THE FIRST TIME
THIS ISN'T HOW I'D PLANNED OUR FIRST MEETING, HAWK.
BUDDA ZING
BUDDA ZING
BARBARA & KARL KESEL • WRITERS
ROB LIEFELD PENCILLER
KARL KESEL INKER
JANICE CHIANG LETTERER
GLENN WHITMORE COLORIST
RENEE WITTERSTAETTER ASSISTANT EDITOR
MIKE CARLIN • EDITOR
SPECIAL THANKS TO KIETH WILLIAMS FOR BACKGROUND ASST.
G-4042

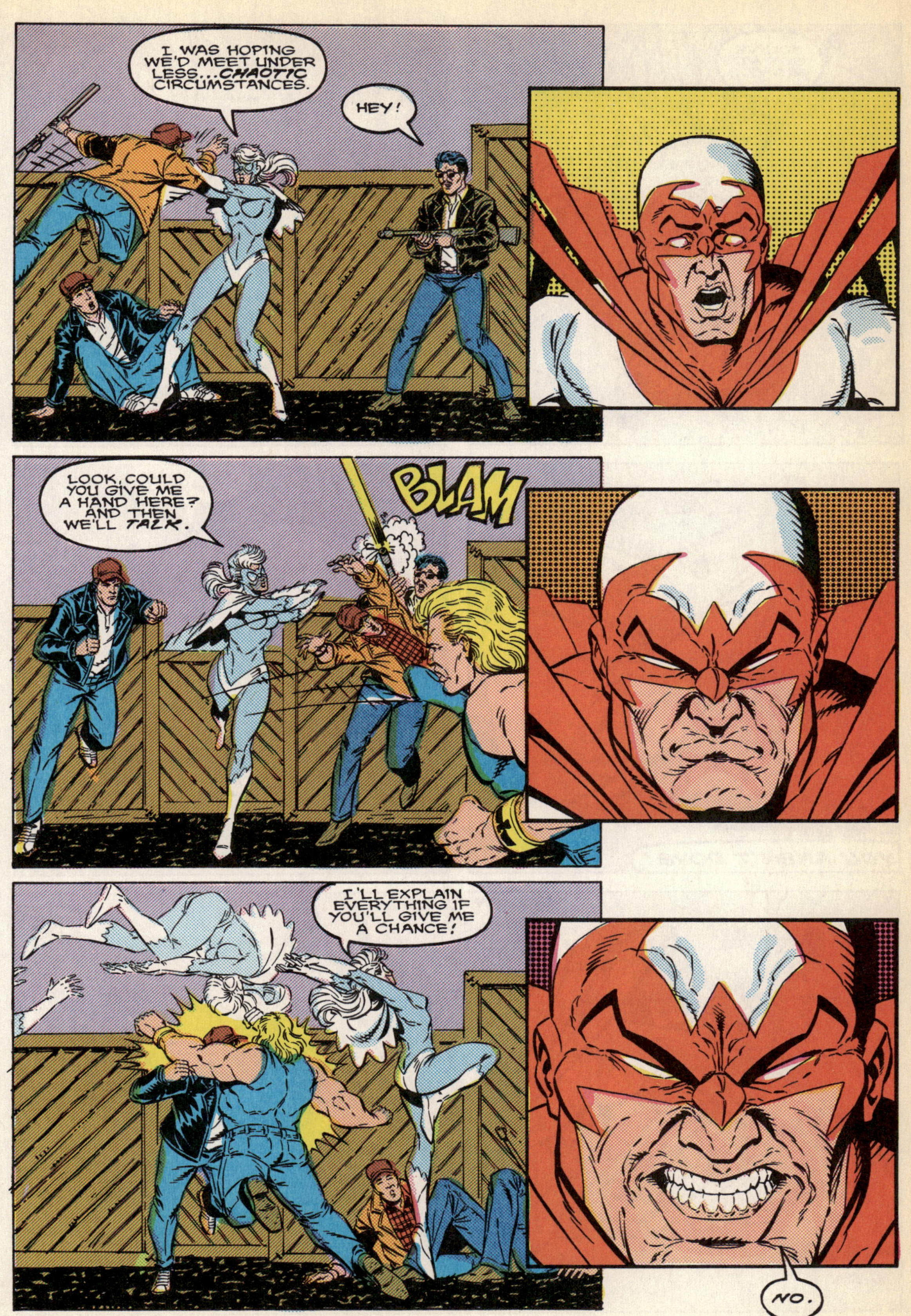
I WAS HOPING WE'D MEET UNDER LESS... CHAOTIC CIRCUMSTANCES.
HEY!
LOOK, COULD YOU GIVE ME A HAND HERE? AND THEN WE'LL TALK.
BLAM
I'LL EXPLAIN EVERYTHING IF YOU'LL GIVE ME A CHANCE!
NO.

YOU'VE GOT NO RIGHT...

WHO DO YOU THINK YOU ARE?

YOU AREN'T DOVE!

YES, I AM, HAWK.
I AM DOVE NOW.

LIAR!
NO ONE CAN EVER BE DOVE AGAIN!

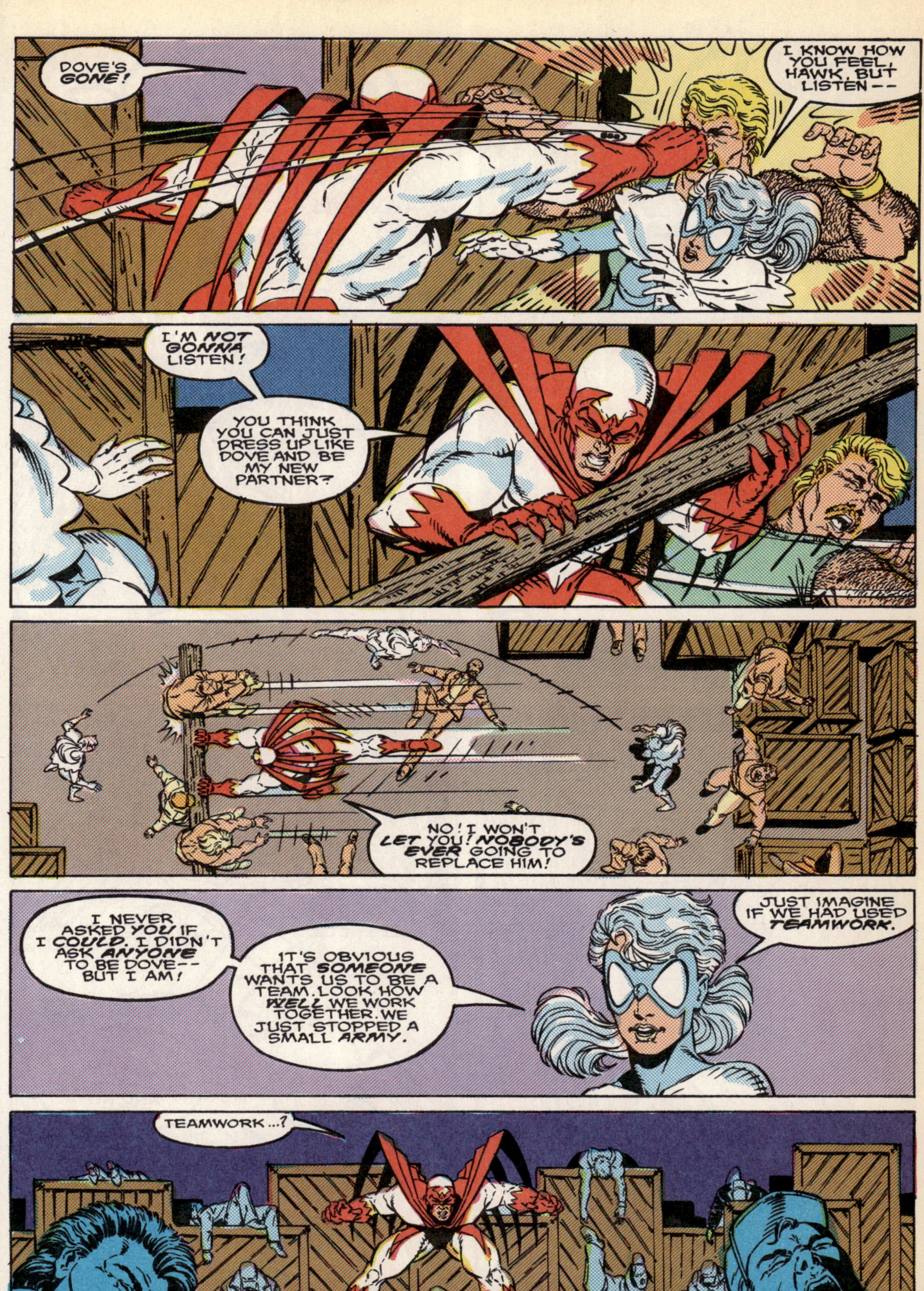

DOVE'S GONE!
I KNOW HOW YOU FEEL, HAWK, BUT LISTEN --
I'M NOT GONNA LISTEN!
YOU THINK YOU CAN JUST DRESS UP LIKE DOVE AND BE MY NEW PARTNER?
NO! I WON'T LET YOU! NOBODY'S EVER GOING TO REPLACE HIM!
I NEVER ASKED YOU IF I COULD. I DIDN'T ASK ANYONE TO BE DOVE-- BUT I AM!
IT'S OBVIOUS THAT SOMEONE WANTS US TO BE A TEAM. LOOK HOW WELL WE WORK TOGETHER. WE JUST STOPPED A SMALL ARMY.
JUST IMAGINE IF WE HAD USED TEAMWORK.
TEAMWORK...?

WE'RE NOT A TEAM.
WE WILL NEVER BE A TEAM!

KA-RRAK
I'M AFRAID THAT DECISION HAS ALREADY BEEN MADE...
FOR THE BOTH OF US!

CAN'T YOU SEE--WE WERE CREATED TO BE A TEAM. WE NEED EACH OTHER!
WHAT'S A HAWK WITHOUT A DOVE?

I DON'T NEED ANYBODY! NOT THE TITANS AND NOT YOU...
...ESPECIALLY NOT YOU!

YOU'RE A THIEF!
I DIDN'T STEAL ANYTHING, HAWK.
THIS WAS GIVEN.
YOU THINK I LIKE THIS ANY BETTER THAN YOU--
UNGH...

HA! YOU WANT TO BE MY PARTNER AND A LITTLE THING LIKE THAT STOPS YOU!
HAWK, IF A LITTLE THING LIKE THAT COULD STOP ME...

...I WOULDN'T BE STOPPING YOU INSTEAD!
SURPRISE!

FLASH

THIS ISN'T JUST A COSTUME I PUT ON ONE DAY, HAWK.
SOMEONE I LOVED WAS IN TROUBLE. A VOICE CAME OUT OF NOWHERE AND OFFERED ME THESE POWERS. I ACCEPTED. SOUND FAMILIAR?
WHENEVER DANGER IS NEAR, I CAN CHANGE INTO DOVE BY SAYING MY NAME, JUST LIKE YOU CHANGE BY SAYING "HAWK".

WHEN THE DANGER IS OVER, I CHANGE BACK.
JUST LIKE YOU.
WHERE ARE YOU?!?

I AM DOVE NOW... THIS ISN'T JUST SOME CHILD-HOOD FANTASY OF MINE. IT MAY NOT BE WHAT EITHER OF US WANTS, HAWK-- THIS IS JUST THE WAY IT IS.

EITHER YOU ACCEPT ME-- AS IS--OR WE'LL NEVER KNOW THE TRUE PURPOSE BEHIND THIS--
SHUT UP! SHUT UP! SHUT UP!

NO ONE CAN TAKE DOVE'S PLACE!
DOVE IS DEAD! DOVE IS DEAD!

NO, HANK...
DON IS DEAD.

...THE AEROTOURIST FLIGHT TO WASHINGTON REPORTED NO TROUBLE AND A TERRORIST BOMB IS SUSPECTED AT THIS TIME...
WE REPEAT, NO SURVIVORS HAVE BEEN FOUND, MAKING THIS THE WORST AIR DISASTER SINCE...
...SEARCHERS REPORT NO SURVIVORS AND REPORT THAT THE VICTIMS SEEM TO BE UNUSUALLY LACERATED BEYOND RECOGNITION...
BACK TO YOU, TOM...
4
HAWK...
RICHMOND
WASHINGTON 105
YOU ARE IN WASHINGTON. I CAN FEEL IT. YOU'RE SO CLOSE...
IT GOT UGLY ON THE PLANE BECAUSE OF YOU, HANK.
I ASKED THEM NICELY TO MAKE THE PLANE GO FASTER...
...BUT THEY LIED. THEY SAID THEY COULDN'T!
I HAD TO SHOW THEM I WAS SERIOUS. DEADLY SERIOUS.
YOU WOULD HAVE BEEN PROUD.
HEY, BUDDY, NEED A LIFT?
YOU HELPING OUT AT THE CRASH? BE MY PLEASURE TO RETURN THE FAVOR.
THANK YOU. YES, I...LENT A HAND.
I HOPE YOU'RE GOING TO WASHINGTON...

...HOW DID SHE KNOW SO MUCH *STUFF* ABOUT ME?
PROBABLY GOT A HOLD OF MY FILE AT TITANS HEADQUARTERS. THOSE GUYS DON'T KNOW THE FIRST THING ABOUT SECURITY!
HANK! OVER HERE!
AND YOU SAID HE WOULDN'T BE UP UNTIL NOON!
I FIGURED JOCKS SLEPT LATE. SO SUE ME.

OH. H'LO, KYLE. GIRLS.
WHOA! LOOKS LIKE YOU HAD A *BAD* NIGHT--YOU GETTING A HEADSTART ON CRAMMING FOR YOUR CALCULUS TESTS?

OKAY, IF I PROMISE NOT TO FLASH YOU AGAIN, WILL YOU STOP LOOKING LIKE SUCH A GRUMP?
FLASH ME?
FLASH*BULB*? FOOTBALL FIELD? I TOOK YOUR PICTURE YESTERDAY?
OH, THAT. FORGOT ALL ABOUT IT, REN.

CHEKHOV, "SOLDIER OF FORTUNE," "GUNS AND AMMO"... JUST WHAT CLASS ARE YOU HEADED FOR, HANK? "REVOLUTION FOR THE PROLETARIAT"?
FLASH?
DOVE FLASHED ME... JUST LIKE *REN* DID!
AND *REN* KNEW ALL ABOUT THE PAULSEN WAREHOUSE!

BUT DAWN AND DONNA WOULD HAVE HEARD ABOUT THAT, TOO.
COURSE, NONE OF THEM HAVE WHITE HAIR...
NOBODY HAS HAIR LIKE THAT! I BET IT'S A *WIG!* YEAH, I BET LOTS OF GIRL HEROES WEAR WIGS!

I THINK IT'S TIME FOR A LITTLE DETECTIVE WORK-- HAWK STYLE!
SORRY I'M SO OUT OF IT, GUYS. I WAS UP LATE STUDYING.
STUDYING? TODAY IS THE FIRST DAY OF CLASSES, HANK!
UH...
PLAYBOOKS, OBVIOUSLY HE HAS TO STAY A STEP AHEAD OF THE FOOTBALL COACH!
RIGHT! THAT'S IT! SO...UH... WHERE WERE YOU LAST NIGHT, DAWN?
EXCUSE ME?
I MEANT... I DIDN'T MEAN... I JUST MEANT THAT I WONDERED WHAT YOUR IDEA OF FUN WAS AT NIGHT.
MY WHAT?
HANK, I THINK WE SHOULD HAVE A LITTLE MAN-TO-MAN TALK ABOUT THE WAY YOU'RE ASKING THIS QUESTION...
I THINK WE SHOULD HAVE A LITTLE GIRL-TO-MAN TALK ABOUT WHY YOU'RE ASKING THIS QUESTION!
HEY, I DIDN'T MEAN TO RILE THE TROOPS. LET'S CHANGE THE SUBJECT...
YES, LET'S.
SO, DONNA-- IS THAT YOUR REAL HAIR?
IS THAT YOUR REAL BRAIN, HANK? HONESTLY, YOU ARE THE STRANGEST...
FIVE TO NINE! ALMOST CLASS TIME, HANK! REN... WHY DON'T YOU WALK HANK THERE?
COME ON, COMRADE, OR THEY'LL START THE REVOLUTION WITHOUT US!
THAT DIDN'T GO QUITE LIKE I PLANNED...

ONCE YOU *RE-ESTABLISH* YOURSELF AS A STUDENT-

BY THE TIME I DO *THAT*--

--YOU'LL HAVE PLENTY OF TIME FOR EXTRA-CURRICULAR ACTIVITIES.

I'LL BE 30! OLD! OVER THE HILL!

GOOD EVENING, JUDGE HALL, MRS. HALL. AND GOOD TO SEE *YOU* AGAIN, MASTER HANK. ARE WE READY TO ORDER?

I THINK SO, GENE. HANK?

I'LL HAVE A CHEESEBURGER AND FRIES.

AMERICAN CHEESE.

CRASH

GOOD LORD!

IT CAME FROM OUTSIDE!

SOMEONE'S SAVING AN OLD LADY FROM THOSE MUGGERS!

ISN'T THAT HAWK'S PARTNER... YOU KNOW... ROBIN?

DOVE.

I THOUGHT DOVE WAS DEAD.
I THOUGHT DOVE WAS A MAN!
WELL, RAE, IT'S HARD TO GET A GOOD LOOK AT DOVE FROM HERE.
I ALWAYS SUSPECTED DOVE WASN'T DEAD. PERHAPS HE'S--OR SHE'S--JUST COME OUT OF RETIREMENT?
I GUESS IT WAS TOO MUCH TO HOPE THAT HAWK AND DOVE'S VIGILANTE JUSTICE WAS GONE FROM WASHINGTON FOR GOOD.
PLEASE... EXCUSE ME... ONE MINUTE.
SHE COULD BE ANYWHERE. FAN OUT--SCAN. PRONTO!
WE GOT THE GRANNY, SHURIKEN--SHE WON'T HASSLE US WITH A HOSTAGE!
SNAP SNAP
RUN AWAY? NO WAY, DUDE. NOT FROM SOME CHICK.
AIN'T NO ORDINARY CHICK WE BE MESSING WITH. SHE BE SOME SUPER-POWER BABE, TAKIN' OUT TRAILER WITH ONE HAN--
YAH--
LOOKING FOR ME?
LAST CHANCE TO GIVE UP PEACEFULLY...
YOU AIN'T IN A POSITION TO BE NAMIN' TERMS, BLUEBIRD.
HIT 'IM IN THE LABANZA, GIRL!
SHUT IT, BAG!
YAHHHHHHHHH!

EXCUSE ME-- CAN I BORROW THIS?
THANKS.
UNGH!

THAT THE BEST YOU CAN DO, BRUCE?
THONK

YOU RELY TOO MUCH ON YOUR WEAPONS. A GOOD FIGHTER WOULDN'T NEED THEM, JUST TRAINING AND AWARENESS.
BUT YOU'RE NOT GOOD FIGHTERS, ARE YOU?

YEAH, YOU KNOW EVERYTHING. YOU'RE A STINKIN' SUPER-HERO. YOU'RE SO WITH IT -- TRY THIS!

WHACK

THAT'S HOW YOU HANDLE SCUM LIKE THIS.
RIGHT AS RAIN, BIG RED! NOW YOU TWO STAND GUARD WHILE I GO FLAG DOWN A FLATFOOT!

YOU FOLLOWED ME HERE, DIDN'T YOU? YOU'VE BEEN SPYING ON ME FOR WEEKS, RIGHT?
THAT'S HOW YOU KNEW SO MUCH ABOUT ME. MY LITTLE SHADOW, HUH?
TELL ME I'M WRONG.

DAMMIT!
LET'S GET ONE THING STRAIGHT: I CAN'T STOP YOU FROM PRETENDING YOU'RE DOVE, BUT I CAN MAKE DAMN SURE YOU DON'T DO IT IN MY TOWN!

GET OUT OF WASHINGTON.
NEVER COME BACK.
IF YOU KNOW WHAT'S GOOD FOR YOU.

BOOK 'EM, DANNO! NOT THE RED ONE, HE'S THE HERO. SHOULDA SEEN HIM SMASH THE TRASH. JUST LIKE **ARNOLD**!

HAWK! MIGHT'VE KNOWN! BUT WHERE'S THIS **WOMAN**...?

FORGET ABOUT HER...

"SO CLOSE...

"AFTER ALL THE MONTHS OF FOLLOWING YOU, HAWK, THE GAP IS CLOSING...
"YOU WERE HERE ONLY HOURS AGO...
"YOU RELAXED WITH... YOUR FAMILY? YOUR WIFE?
"A LITTLE BIRD TOLD ME.
"IF I ONLY KNEW WHO YOU WERE, HAWK, EVERYTHING WOULD BE SO MUCH SIMPLER AND LESS... PAINFUL.

"WHEN YOU'RE HAWK, YOU'RE A BEACON TO ME. A MAGNET. WHEN YOU CHANGE BACK TO YOUR HUMAN FORM, YOU COULD BE ANYONE.
"NEW YORK, MEXICO, NICARAGUA... I WASTED SO MUCH TIME...
"AND NOW MY TIME'S RUN OUT.
"YOU'VE ALREADY MET DOVE.

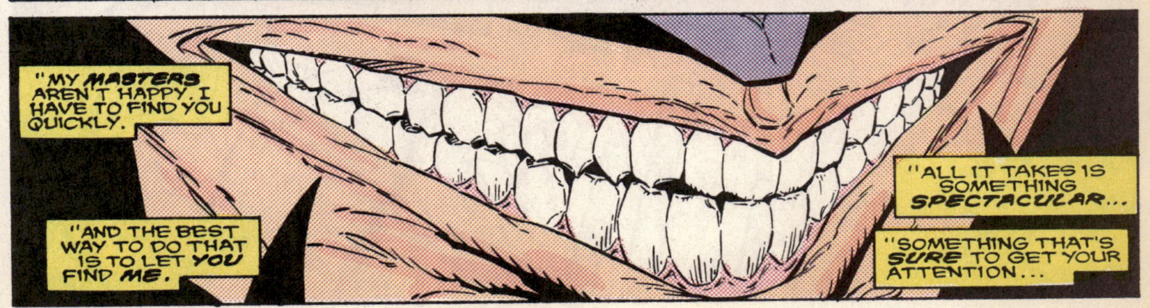
"MY MASTERS AREN'T HAPPY. I HAVE TO FIND YOU QUICKLY.
"AND THE BEST WAY TO DO THAT IS TO LET YOU FIND ME.
"ALL IT TAKES IS SOMETHING SPECTACULAR...
"SOMETHING THAT'S SURE TO GET YOUR ATTENTION...

"... I HOPE YOU ARE PROPERLY IMPRESSED!"
Le Parc

WHOEVER DID THIS WORKED FAST, DETECTIVE. GUTTED THE ALARM SYSTEM WITH SOMETHING THAT CAN SLICE THROUGH METAL.
THERE'S OVER SEVENTY PEOPLE DEAD IN THERE. DOESN'T LOOK LIKE ANYONE GOT OUT ALIVE.
SEEMS TO HAVE HAPPENED BETWEEN ELEVEN AND ELEVEN-THIRTY. UNFORTUNATELY, THEY WERE STILL CROWDED.
I HATE TO SAY IT, KIDS...

...BUT IT LOOKS LIKE THE SPECIAL CRIMES UNIT IS GONNA BE BUSY.
I JUST HOPE ONE PERSON DIDN'T DO ALL THIS...
AND I HOPE THAT HAWK DOESN'T GET INVOLVED...
OR ISN'T INVOLVED ALREADY...

HEY, KYLE! DONNA! OVER HERE! WANNA JOIN ME FOR SOME BREAKFAST? JUICE? DONUTS?
WELL, UH...
SURE WE WILL, HANK.

THEN YOU'RE NOT STILL MAD AT ME, DONNA?
HOW COULD I BE MAD AT YOU, HANK? YOU'RE ONE OF THE FUNNIEST GUYS I KNOW!
GREAT! THEN BREAKFAST IS ON ME!
DON'T TEMPT ME...

HOLD THE PHONE, FOLKS! I HAVE SOMEONE HERE IN SERIOUS NEED OF CAFFEINE!

REN? YOU'RE KIDDING RIGHT, LITTLE MISS HYPERTENSION IN NEED OF MORE ZING?
I'VE BEEN UP ALL NIGHT COVERING A MASSACRE AT "LE PARC." JUST GOT OUT OF THE DARKROOM. HOPE THE PICTURES MAKE OUR PAPER, AT LEAST.
LOOK!

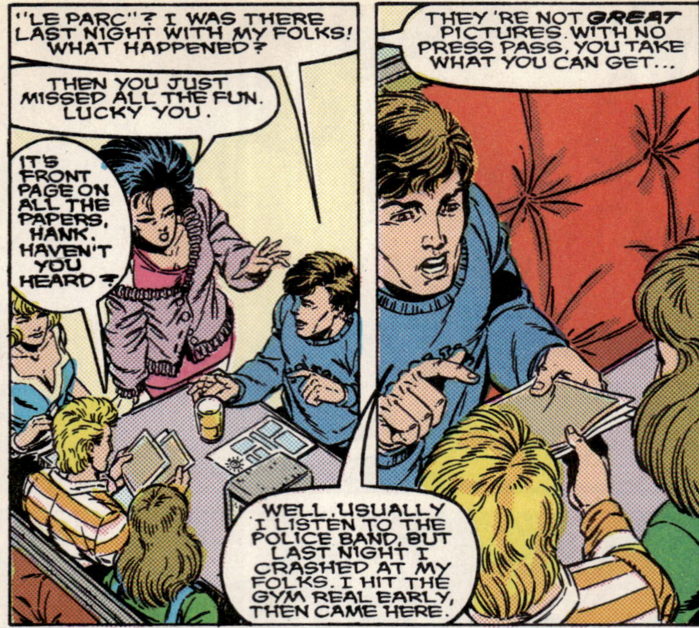
"LE PARC"? I WAS THERE LAST NIGHT WITH MY FOLKS! WHAT HAPPENED?
THEN YOU JUST MISSED ALL THE FUN. LUCKY YOU.
IT'S FRONT PAGE ON ALL THE PAPERS, HANK. HAVEN'T YOU HEARD?
THEY'RE NOT GREAT PICTURES. WITH NO PRESS PASS, YOU TAKE WHAT YOU CAN GET...
WELL, USUALLY I LISTEN TO THE POLICE BAND, BUT LAST NIGHT I CRASHED AT MY FOLKS. I HIT THE GYM REAL EARLY, THEN CAME HERE.

THIS ONE IS VERY GOOD, REN. REALLY CAPTURES THE EMOTION.
AND LOOK AT THE ODD BRACELET IN THE BAG. I'VE NEVER SEEN ANYTHING LIKE IT.
IS THAT EGYPTIAN? NO, ASIAN...

I JUST REMEMBERED... I HAVE TO GO SOMEWHERE!
GO? BUT YOU SAID YOU WERE BUYING BREAKFAST, HANK!
WELL, I'LL JUST LEAVE SOME MONEY AND...
WHERE'S MY WALLET?

I LEFT IT AT MY FOLKS' HOUSE! THAT'S WHERE I HAVE TO GO-- TO MY FOLKS' HOUSE TO GET MY WALLET!
IS IT JUST ME OR IS HE MAKING ABSOLUTELY NO SENSE TO THE REST OF YOU EITHER?

COULDN'T TELL THEM THAT I'VE SEEN THAT BIRD WRISTBAND A LOT RECENTLY-- ON PEOPLE TRYING TO KILL ME!
THIS WAREHOUSE IS STILL MY BEST LEAD.
I DON'T KNOW WHAT THESE PUNKS ARE UP TO...

...BUT A LITTLE HEAD-BASHING COULDN'T HURT 'EM ANY!
I CAN'T WAIT TO SEE THEIR FACES WHEN I--
LOOKIN' FOR SOMETHIN', COLLEGE BOY?
GEORGETOWN

HUH!?
WHERE'D THESE GUYS COME FROM?
QUITE THE CONVERSATIONALIST, AIN'T HE?
PROBABLY LIKE TO TALK WITH THE BOSS, THOUGH.
DON'T THINK THEY MEAN SPRINGSTEEN! BETTER SAY THE WORD AND CHANGE TO HAWK RIGHT AWAY!

--TAKE HIM!
HA--
CRACK

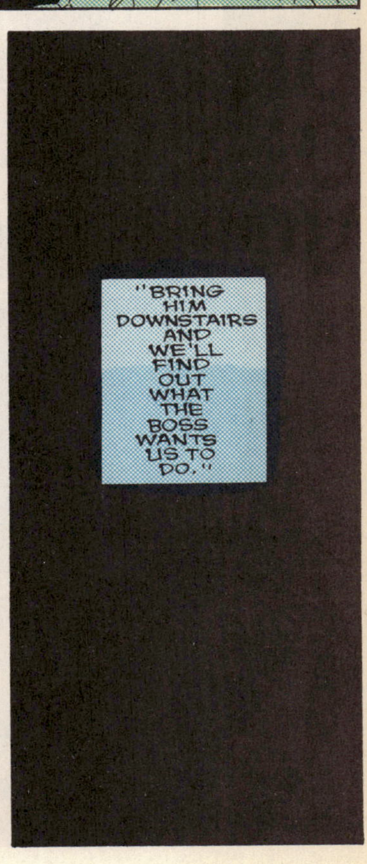
"BRING HIM DOWNSTAIRS AND WE'LL FIND OUT WHAT THE BOSS WANTS US TO DO."

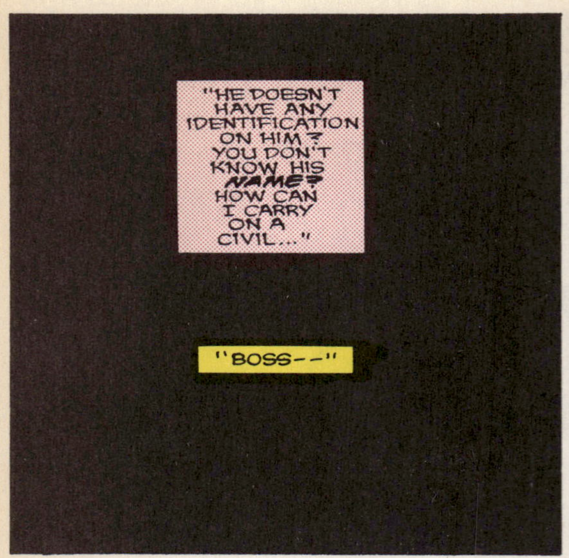
"HE DOESN'T HAVE ANY IDENTIFICATION ON HIM? YOU DON'T KNOW HIS NAME? HOW CAN I CARRY ON A CIVIL..."
"BOSS--"

--HE'S AWAKE.
GET OUT.
EVERYONE GET OUT.

GREETINGS.
I'M SORRY TO SAY I DON'T KNOW YOUR NAME, SO I CAN'T GIVE YOU A PROPER WELCOME.
A MINOR POINT, YOU MAY THINK, BUT NOT TO ME.
I BELIEVE IN THE POWER OF NAMES. LEGEND HAS IT THAT EVERYTHING, EVERYONE HAS TWO NAMES...

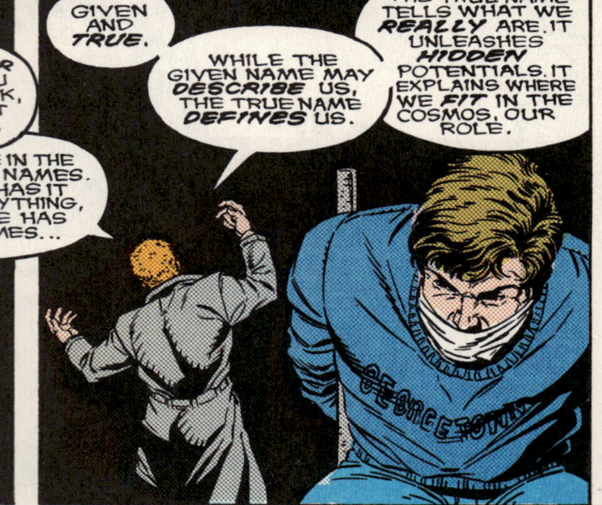
GIVEN AND TRUE.
WHILE THE GIVEN NAME MAY DESCRIBE US, THE TRUE NAME DEFINES US.
THE TRUE NAME TELLS WHAT WE REALLY ARE. IT UNLEASHES HIDDEN POTENTIALS. IT EXPLAINS WHERE WE FIT IN THE COSMOS, OUR ROLE.

BUILDER OR DESTROYER. ANGEL OR DEMON.
ORDER OR CHAOS.
I GO BY MANY TITLES, BUT MY TRUE NAME IS KESTREL.

AND YOU, MY FRIEND...
...WHAT IS YOUR TRUE NAME?
TO BE CONTINUED...

DC
HAWK & DOVE™
3
DEC 88
U.S. $1.00
CAN $1.35
APPROVED BY THE COMICS CODE AUTHORITY
FIVE ISSUE MINI-SERIES
Y KESEL,
IEFELD &
ESEL
KESTREL COMES...
KESTREL KILLS!

THE AIR AND SPACE MUSEUM, WASHINGTON, D.C.-- A MONUMENT TO MAN'S MASTERY OF THE SKY--
EVERY DAY THOUSANDS COME TO MARVEL AT EVIDENCE SHOWING THAT MAN HAS DARED TO TAKE THE SECRETS OF BIRDS AND MAKE THEM HIS OWN...
ROCKETS THAT STREAK FASTER THAN SOUND...
IRON BIRDS MORE DESTRUCTIVE THAN ANY CREATURE OF EARTH...
AGENTS OF CHAOS... OUT OF CONTROL!
BARBARA AND KARL KESEL • WRITERS
RON LIEFELD • PENCILLER
KARL KESEL • INKER
JANICE CHIANG • LETTERER
GLENN WHITMORE • COLORIST
RENÉE WITTERSTAETER - ASSISTANT EDITOR • MIKE CARLIN - EDITOR

YES, HAWK-- THAT'S IT!
I'VE SEARCHED FOR YOU TOO LONG TO HAVE OUR MEETING END TOO QUICKLY!
BUDDY, YOU LIKED THAT...

...YOU'LL LOVE THIS!

AS FOR OUR "MEETING"--
MEETING ADJOURNED!
KRAK

HOLY...!
I BROKE MY HAND.
I BROKE MY HAND!

POWER. STRENGTH. RAGE.
YOU'RE EVERYTHING THE MASTERS PROMISED, HAWK.
NOW LET ME SHOW YOU WHAT I CAN DO.

WHAT'S THIS GUY MADE OF?
WHY'RE ALL THE FRUITCAKES AFTER ME THIS WEEK?
FIRST THAT BOGUS DOVE BIMBO SHOWS UP, AND THEN THIS LUNATIC KIDNAPS ME...

...MY NAME IS KESTREL.

AND YOU, MY FRIEND, WHAT IS YOUR TRUE NAME?
IS IT... HAWK?

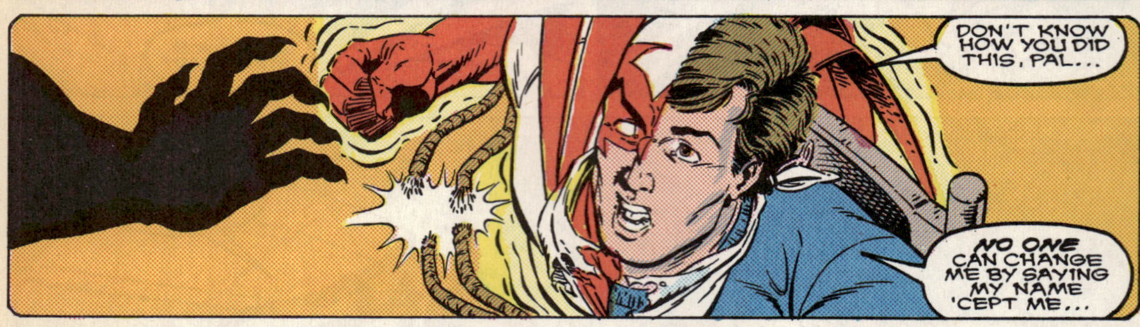
DON'T KNOW HOW YOU DID THIS, PAL...
NO ONE CAN CHANGE ME BY SAYING MY NAME 'CEPT ME...

NOT THAT I'M SORRY...
NO, YOU'RE THE ONE THAT'S GONNA BE SORRY!

DO YOU LIKE BEING BEAT ON, KESTREL?
THIS KIND OF CONFRONTATION REALLY CHARGE YOU UP?
VERY CLEVER, HAWK!

YOU DO SEEM TO BE ENJOYING THIS.
BUT NOT AS MUCH AS I AM.

SKRAK-AK-KOOM!

IMPRESSED, HAWK?
THAT'S NOTHING COMPARED TO YOUR POTENTIAL BROTHER. THE MASTERS AND I COULD TEACH YOU SO MANY THINGS!
YEAH... WELL...

I'VE ALWAYS BEEN A LOUSY STUDENT!

AAAAAAAAH!

YOU'LL PAY FOR THIS, HAWK! THE LORDS OF CHAOS AREN'T TO BE TRIFLED WITH!

YOU MEAN I'M BEING SENT TO THE PRINCIPAL'S OFFICE *AGAIN*?

GOTTA END THIS *FAST!* THIS GUY'S A TOUGH CUSTOMER-- ALTHOUGH I'VE BEEN IN *WORSE* SITUATIONS.

I THINK.

SNAP

YO! PEOPLE! HAUL IT! GET OUTTA HERE!

I SAID... *MOVE!*

WHAT'RE YOU *DOING?* THAT MODEL WAS PRICELESS!
SO NOW IT'S *MODERN ART.* YOU'LL MAKE A FORTUNE.
YEAH... AND *YOU'LL* PAY!
EVERYONE'S A CRITIC.

OW! OW! OW!
I GOTTA GET OUTTA SIGHT. WITH THE DANGER OVER, I'LL BE CHANGING BACK TO HANK HALL SOON.

AAAAGH!
UUUUNHH--!
DAMN! HE HURT ME *BAD!*
FUNNY--IT'S TAKING ME A LONG TIME TO CHANGE BACK...
I HOPE THAT--

LOOK OUT!
OH, MY GOD!
HUH?
KAPOW
KAPOW
AAAIIIEEEEE!
DON'T TELL ME--

I DON'T BELIEVE WE WERE FINISHED, HAWK.

THERE SHE IS!
I'M SAVED!

PLEASE BE MERCIFUL! TAKE PITY ON A CHEESEHEAD WHO'S BEEN UP ALL NIGHT AND JUST WANTS TO SLEEEEEP...!
REN!
DAWN... WHAT?
SHE... UH... LOCKED HERSELF OUT OF YOUR APARTMENT.

AGAIN? LUCKILY, ROOMIE, I HAVE MY SPARE KEY... AS ALWAYS!
I HAVE EIGHT SPARE KEYS, DONNA...
...BACK AT THE APARTMENT...

AND YOU WANT TO ROMANCE HANK HALL, THE MAN WHO MAKES STALLONE LOOK INTELLECTUAL!
CHILL OUT, DONNA! HANK'S NO EINSTEIN, BUT--
HANK HAS NOT LED A LIFE OF COUNTRY CLUBS AND TENNIS SETS LIKE SOME PEOPLE, MS. CABOT!

MY MOTHER'S A DIPLOMATIC COURIER. SHE TOLD ME THAT HANK WAS A POLITICAL PRISONER IN NICARAGUA.
RIGHT OR WRONG, HE BELIEVED IN A CAUSE AND ALMOST PAID FOR IT WITH HIS LIFE.

IS THAT SOMETHING YOU WOULD DO, DONNA?
...POLICE CORDONED OFF THE AIR AND SPACE MUSEUM--
--WHERE THE SUPER-HERO HAWK IS BATTLING WITH AN UNKNOWN FOE...
CASUALTIES AND DAMAGES ARE HIGH...

I ADMIRE YOUR STUBBORNNESS, HAWK. I'M SURE THAT'S ONE OF THE REASONS THEY CHOSE YOU.
BUT LOOK AT YOU NOW.
THERE'S STILL TIME TO SAVE YOU, HAWK.

JOIN ME AND MY MASTERS.
I DON'T NEED--
AAARGH!
--ANYONE!

YOU'LL COME AROUND, HAWK. YOU'LL REALIZE THAT A MAN WHO SERVES BOTH HOUSES HAS NO POWER.

NO ORDER. NO CHAOS.
NO COHESION, ONLY CONFUSION.

NO NAME...

...NO CONTROL!

AAAAAAHHH.

I REALLY DIDN'T WANT TO KILL YOU, HAWK.
BUT WE'RE HAVING SUCH A GOOD TIME...

WHY STOP NOW?

DON'T YOU LAY ANOTHER HAND ON HIM.

ABOUT TIME YOU SHOWED UP. I WAS GETTING TIRED OF PLAYING WITH HIM...
...AND I WANTED TO MEET THE NEW DOVE.
I'VE BEEN CURIOUS...

WHO ARE YOU?
MY NAME IS KESTREL. I'M A MESSENGER. AN ADVISOR. ONCE HAWK LISTENS TO ME--
--I'LL BE HIS NEW PARTNER.
NEVER.

YOU DON'T UNDERSTAND, DOVE...
WHEN I'M THROUGH WITH YOU, HE WON'T HAVE ANY ALTERNATIVE!

NOT IF THAT'S THE BEST YOU CAN DO--
TRUST ME, DOVE--

--I HAVEN'T EVEN BEGUN TO FIGHT!

NEITHER HAVE I!
I DON'T WORK ONE STEP AT A TIME, LIKE HAWK DOES... I GET THE BIG PICTURE.

YOU ARE GOOD, DOVE--BUT MY MASTERS HAVE BEEN FIGHTING YOUR MASTERS FOR MILLENNIA...
AND WE ALWAYS WIN.
IN THE END, EVERYTHING ALWAYS GIVES WAY TO CHAOS!

NOTHING WILL EVER CHANGE THAT! NOT YOU!
NOT THE EXPERIMENT!
HAWK AND DOVE... HA!

I DON'T KNOW WHAT YOU'RE BABBLING ABOUT, KESTREL.
MASTERS. MILLENNIA. CHAOS. IT MAKES NO SENSE.
TO ME, YOU'RE JUST ANOTHER LUNATIC IN A COSTUME.

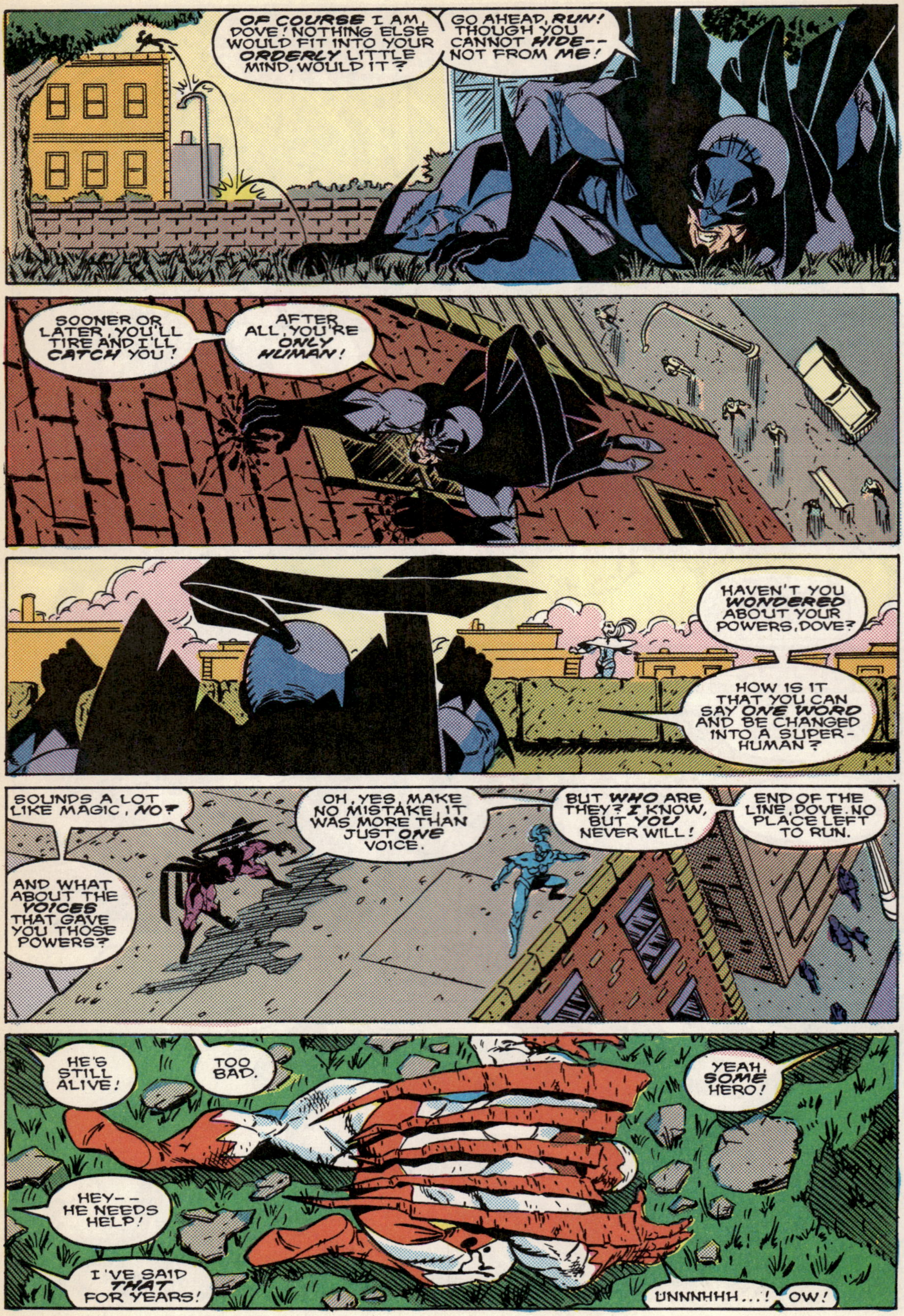

OF COURSE I AM, DOVE! NOTHING ELSE WOULD FIT INTO YOUR ORDERLY LITTLE MIND, WOULD IT?

GO AHEAD, RUN! THOUGH YOU CANNOT HIDE-- NOT FROM ME!

SOONER OR LATER, YOU'LL TIRE AND I'LL CATCH YOU!

AFTER ALL, YOU'RE ONLY HUMAN!

HAVEN'T YOU WONDERED ABOUT YOUR POWERS, DOVE?

HOW IS IT THAT YOU CAN SAY ONE WORD AND BE CHANGED INTO A SUPER-HUMAN?

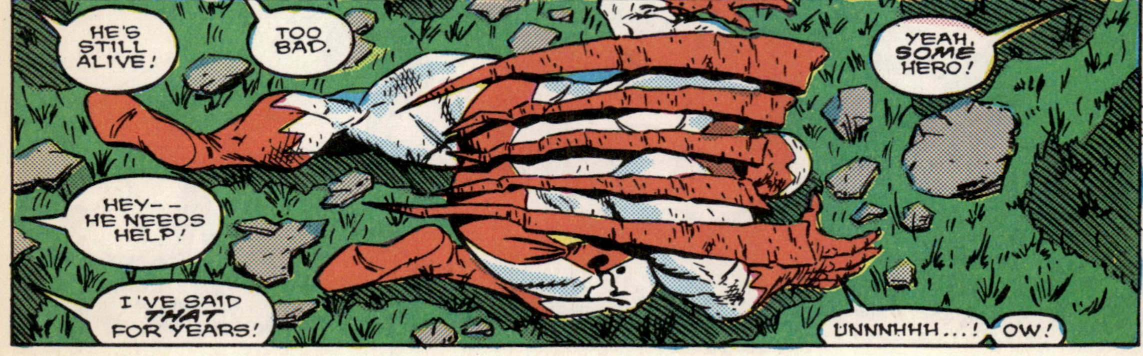

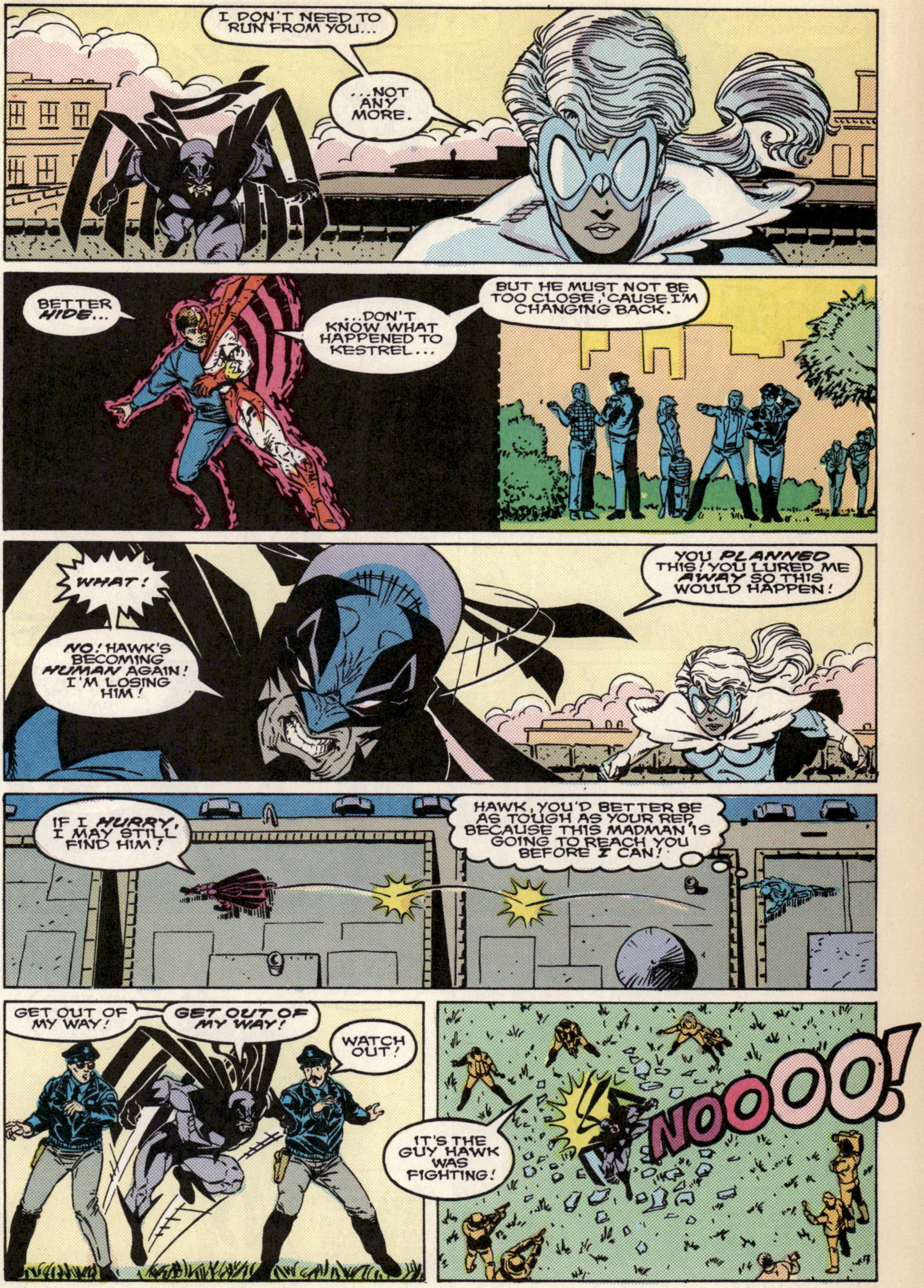

I DON'T NEED TO RUN FROM YOU...
...NOT ANY MORE.

BETTER HIDE...
...DON'T KNOW WHAT HAPPENED TO KESTREL...
BUT HE MUST NOT BE TOO CLOSE, 'CAUSE I'M CHANGING BACK.

DOVE! YOU'LL DIE FOR THIS!
HE'S HEADIN' BACK, CAPTAIN.
HIT 'IM WITH THE TEAR GAS, WOLFSON!
GET THE BIG GUNS READY!

POOM! POOM!

WIND'S TAKIN' THE GAS SOUTH! BOYER-- CLEAR OUT THE CIVILIANS OVER THERE!
MASON! LAZLO! BE READY FOR ANYTHING!

HE'S-- HE'S GONE, CAPTAIN!
GONE? KESTREL MUST HAVE CHANGED LIKE WE DO AND SLIPPED AWAY IN THE CROWD.
AND I'M IN NO CONDITION TO LOOK FOR HIM--!
HANK! WHAT HAPPENED TO YOU?

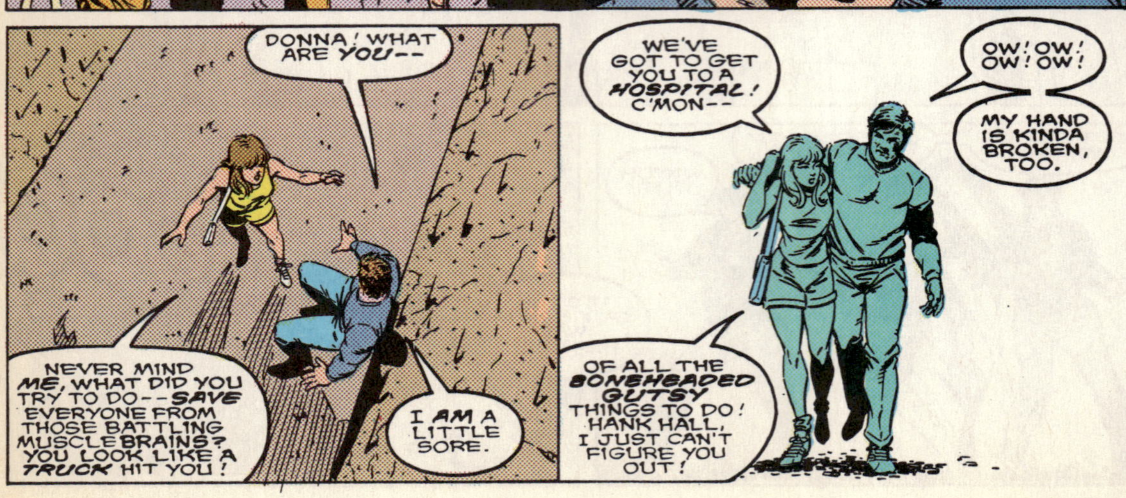
DONNA! WHAT ARE YOU--
NEVER MIND ME, WHAT DID YOU TRY TO DO--SAVE EVERYONE FROM THOSE BATTLING MUSCLEBRAINS? YOU LOOK LIKE A TRUCK HIT YOU!
I AM A LITTLE SORE.
WE'VE GOT TO GET YOU TO A HOSPITAL! C'MON--
OW! OW! OW! OW!
MY HAND IS KINDA BROKEN, TOO.
OF ALL THE BONEHEADED GUTSY THINGS TO DO! HANK HALL, I JUST CAN'T FIGURE YOU OUT!

THAT NIGHT...
EVERYONE POPS BAIL AND WALKS, 'CEPT ME.
I SCREW UP ONE JOB AND I'M POISON.
THAT OLD BAG WAS EASY MONEY. WHO KNEW SUPER-CREEPS WOULD SHOW?
BUT I'LL SHOW 'EM, AND NO ONE'LL EVER CALL ME A KID AGAIN.

HELLO, SHADOWBLADE.
THAT IS WHAT YOU LIKE TO BE CALLED, ISN'T IT?
I HEAR YOU HAD A RUN-IN WITH HAWK AND DOVE YESTERDAY.*
KANK!
HOW WOULD YOU LIKE TO EVEN THE SCORE?
*LAST ISSUE.

BEST OFFER IN WEEKS, MAN! JUST SET ME UP AND LET ME LOOSE.
EXACTLY. FOLLOW ME AND KEEP UP. IF YOU FALL BEHIND, I'M NOT WAITING.

I LIKE YOUR STYLE, MAN. CLOSE THE DEAL, MOVE ON UP. DON'T MESS WITH WORDS. DON'T MESS WITH KEYS...
I DIDN'T HAVE TIME FOR KEYS...

...I WAS BUSY.
SLICK! NOW THIS-- THIS IS DOIN' REAL BUSINESS.

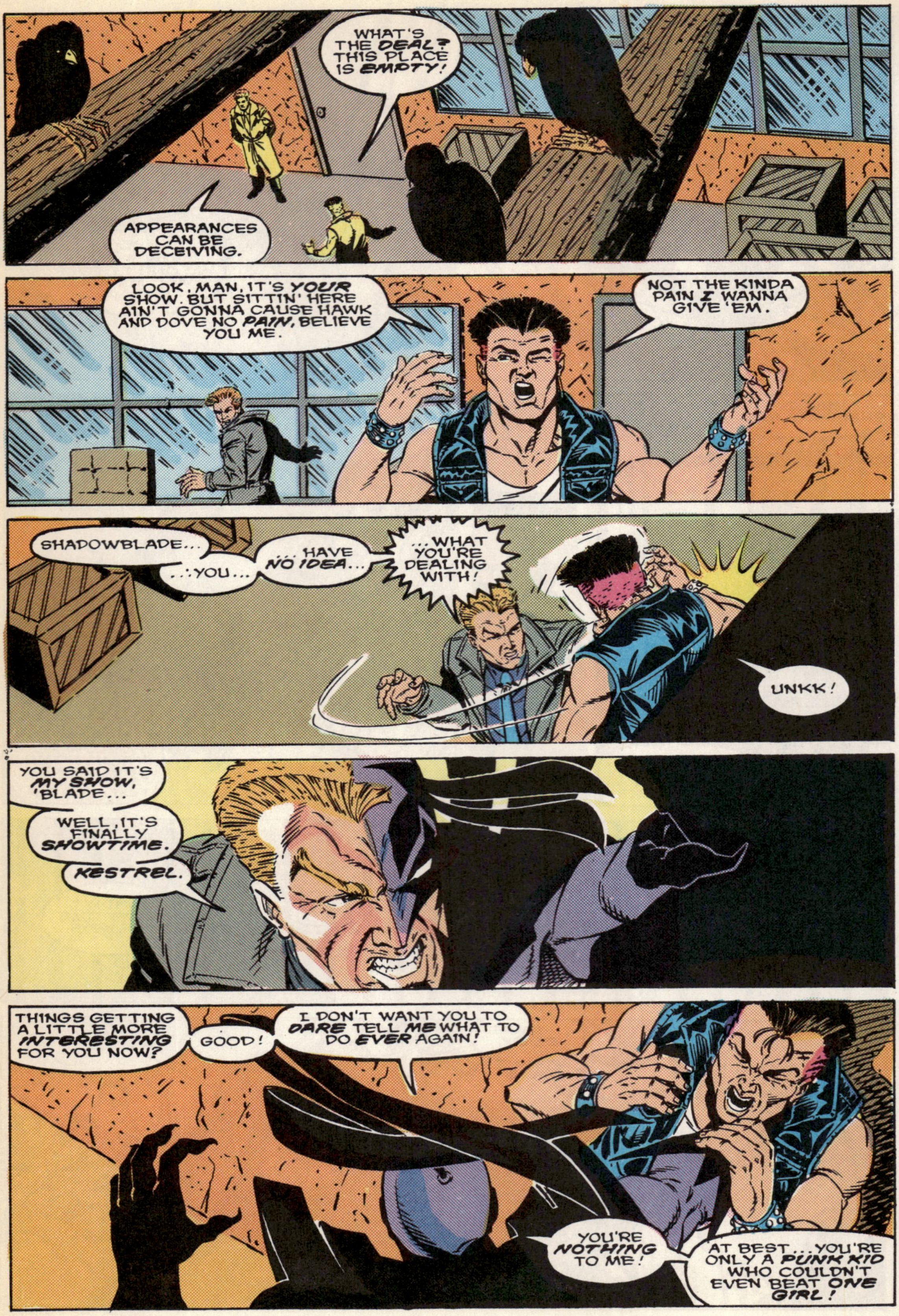

WHAT'S THE ***DEAL?*** THIS PLACE IS ***EMPTY!***
APPEARANCES CAN BE DECEIVING.

LOOK, MAN, IT'S ***YOUR*** SHOW. BUT SITTIN' HERE AIN'T GONNA CAUSE HAWK AND DOVE NO ***PAIN***, BELIEVE YOU ME.
NOT THE KINDA PAIN ***I*** WANNA GIVE 'EM.

SHADOWBLADE...
...YOU...
...HAVE ***NO IDEA***...
...WHAT YOU'RE DEALING WITH!
UNKK!

BUT HAWK--
HAWK IS MINE!

I CAN GET YOU POWER... MAKE SURE NO ONE EVER TREATS YOU LIKE A CHILD AGAIN... AND YOU CAN DO WHATEVER YOU LIKE TO DOVE.
BUT LEAVE HAWK TO ME, OR I'LL PEEL YOUR SKULL LIKE A GRAPE.
NOW. YOU WANT POWER...?
JUST WALK THROUGH THAT DOOR.

SCARED?
GO TO HELL.

AFTER YOU.

BREAK OUT THE HEAVY ARTILLERY, BOYS. GOT A JOB FOR YOU.
THIS SHOULD FLUSH OUT HAWK AND TAKE CARE OF DOVE AT THE SAME TIME.
AAAIIIEEEEEEEEE!
YOU FIND OUT WHO HAWK IS, BOSS?
NO, I DON'T KNOW WHO...

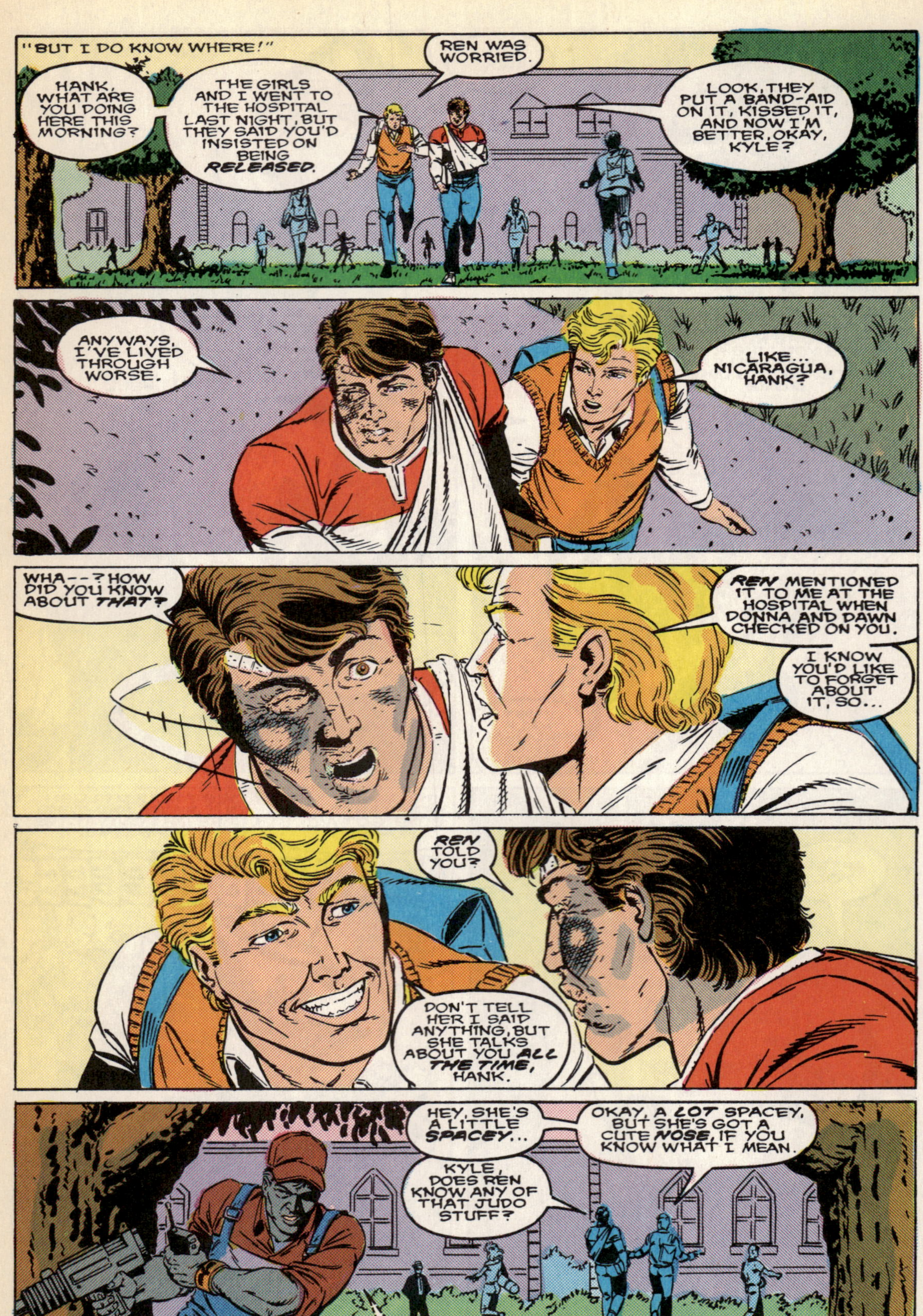
"BUT I DO KNOW WHERE!"
REN WAS WORRIED.
HANK, WHAT ARE YOU DOING HERE THIS MORNING?
THE GIRLS AND I WENT TO THE HOSPITAL LAST NIGHT, BUT THEY SAID YOU'D INSISTED ON BEING RELEASED.
LOOK, THEY PUT A BAND-AID ON IT, KISSED IT, AND NOW I'M BETTER, OKAY, KYLE?
ANYWAYS, I'VE LIVED THROUGH WORSE.
LIKE... NICARAGUA, HANK?
WHA--? HOW DID YOU KNOW ABOUT THAT?
REN MENTIONED IT TO ME AT THE HOSPITAL WHEN DONNA AND DAWN CHECKED ON YOU.
I KNOW YOU'D LIKE TO FORGET ABOUT IT, SO...
REN TOLD YOU?
DON'T TELL HER I SAID ANYTHING, BUT SHE TALKS ABOUT YOU ALL THE TIME, HANK.
HEY, SHE'S A LITTLE SPACEY...
OKAY, A LOT SPACEY, BUT SHE'S GOT A CUTE NOSE, IF YOU KNOW WHAT I MEAN.
KYLE, DOES REN KNOW ANY OF THAT JUDO STUFF?
NOW.

BOOM
KYLE-- DOWN!

WHAT THE--!
SOME SORT OF COMMANDO ATTACK--
BUT THESE AREN'T THE TACTICS OF ANY GROUP I KNOW ABOUT!

ARE YOU OKAY?
OW!
JUST MY DAMN HAND--
KYLE-- I GOTTA FIND REN... RIGHT NOW!

SHE'S WORKING THE A.M. SHIFT AT SUDS, BUT YOU CAN'T GET ACROSS CAMPUS IN THIS--
SURE I CAN!
BUT YOU--STICK LOW AND CLOSE TO THE WALL AND GET OUT OF HERE FAST! DON'T CROSS ANY OPEN AREAS!
GO!

BA-KOOM
BRAT-AT-AT-A

PRETTY SURE I SAW RAVEN-BRACELETS ON SOME OF THESE GOONS...
...THAT MAKES THIS ONE OF KESTREL'S LITTLE GAMES.
DON'T WORRY, MR. SLICE-N-DICE--YOU WANT ME, YOU GOT ME...
BUT ON MY TERMS!
UH-OH! THAT GUY LEADIN' THIS PACK...
...AIN'T KESTREL!
REMEMBER ME, MR. HAWK AND DOVE? THE KID WITH THE OLD LADY IN THE PARK?
I'M BACK-- BIGGER AND BETTER THAN EVER!
NOW IT'S A FAIR FIGHT, SUPER-DUDES! AND SHADOWBLADE IS GONNA GRIND YOUR BONES TO DUST!

DC
4
WINTER
U.S.$1.00
CAN $1.35
APPROVED BY THE COMICS CODE AUTHORITY
HAWK & DOVE™
FIVE ISSUE MINI-SERIES
BY KESEL, LIEFELD & KESEL

HEY, HAWK AND DOVE-- C'MON OUT AND PLAY!
DON'T LET THE OUTFIT FOOL YA! IT'S YER OLD BUDDY FROM THE PARK! I MUGGED THAT OLD LADY... REMEMBER?

MET A FRIEND OF YOURS... MAN CALLED KESTREL... AND HE SET ME UP REAL FINE!
AIN'T NO KID YOU BE FACING THIS TIME, HEROES... NOW I GOT THE POWER TO TAKE YOU OUT!

THIS IS SHADOWBLADE TALKIN' AT YA!
AND I'LL FIND YOU TWO EVEN IF ME AND MY MEN HAVE TO TEAR DOWN ALL OF GEORGETOWN TO DO IT!

REN, OL' GAL, THIS BOZO IS A MANIAC...
AND YOUR TICKET TO A PULITZER PRIZE!
FILM, DON'T FAIL ME NOW!

OOOOWW!

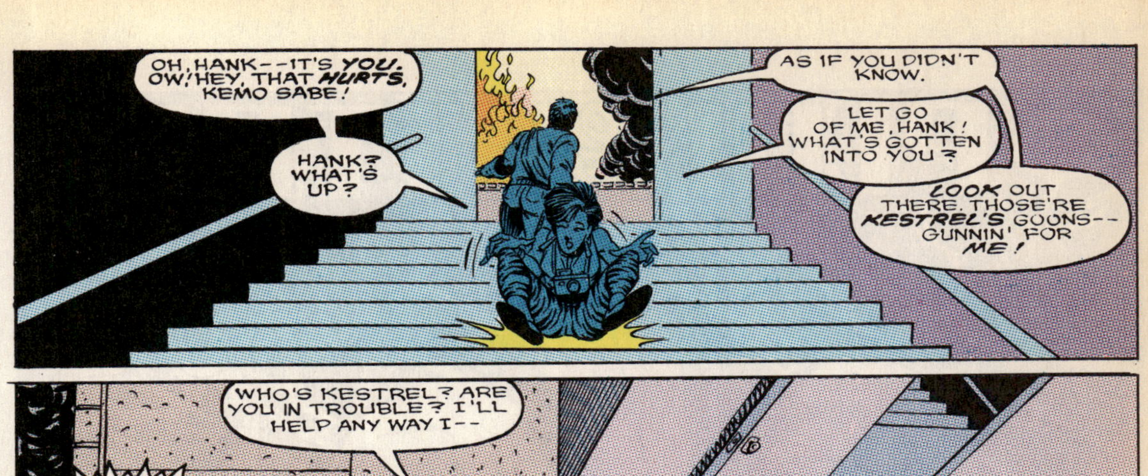
OH, HANK--IT'S YOU. OW! HEY, THAT HURTS, KEMO SABE!
HANK? WHAT'S UP?
AS IF YOU DIDN'T KNOW.
LET GO OF ME, HANK! WHAT'S GOTTEN INTO YOU?
LOOK OUT THERE. THOSE'RE KESTREL'S GOONS-- GUNNIN' FOR ME!

WHO'S KESTREL? ARE YOU IN TROUBLE? I'LL HELP ANY WAY I--
DON'T ACT STUPID!
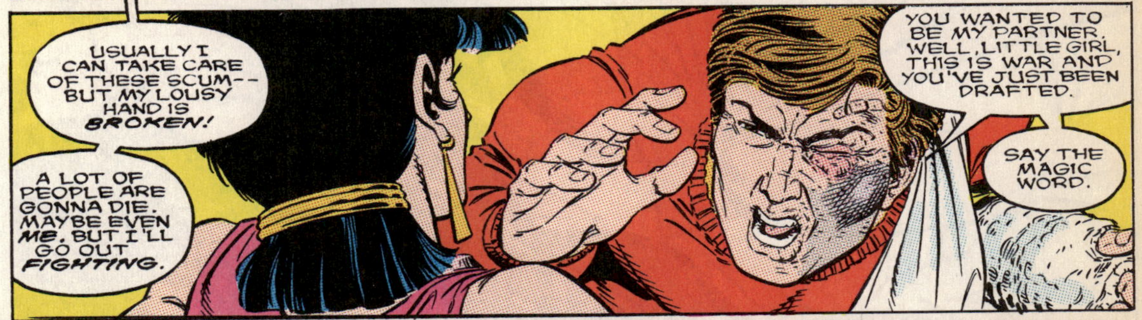
USUALLY I CAN TAKE CARE OF THESE SCUM-- BUT MY LOUSY HAND IS BROKEN!
A LOT OF PEOPLE ARE GONNA DIE. MAYBE EVEN ME. BUT I'LL GO OUT FIGHTING.
YOU WANTED TO BE MY PARTNER. WELL, LITTLE GIRL, THIS IS WAR AND YOU'VE JUST BEEN DRAFTED.
SAY THE MAGIC WORD.

YOU'RE ACTING CRAZY, HANK. I DON'T KNOW--
SAY IT!
I DON'T KNOW WHAT YOU WANT ME TO SAY, HANK! TELL ME WHAT YOU WANT ME TO SAY!
FINE! I'LL GO FIRST!

HAWK!

YOUR TURN!
PLAN OF ATTACK
HAWK & DOVE
BARBARA & KARL KESEL • WRITERS
ROB LIEFELD • PENCILLER
KARL KESEL • INKER
JANICE CHIANG • LETTERER
GLENN WHITMORE • COLORIST
RENÉE WITTERSTAETTER - ASSISTANT EDITOR • MIKE CARLIN - EDITOR

QUIT PLAYIN' GAMES!
HAWK... HAWK...
HAWK...

LET HER GO.
I'M THE ONE YOU WANT.

ARE YOU ALL RIGHT, REN?
YEAH...SURE...THIS HAPPENS TO ME ALL THE TIME!
I THOUGHT SHE WAS DOVE. SHE KNEW ABOUT NICARAGUA.

I TOLD HER ABOUT THAT. ALL THIS IS MY FAULT FOR TRYING TO BE SO CLEVER.
GOT THAT RIGHT.

WE'LL TALK ABOUT THAT LATER. RIGHT NOW WE HAVE KESTREL'S ARMY TO WORRY ABOUT.
HOW'S YOUR HAND?
LIKE I SAID: BROKEN. BUT I HEAL PRETTY QUICK WHEN I'M HAWK, SO DON'T WORRY ABOUT ME.

THEN THE FIRST THING WE HAVE TO DO IS GET AS MANY INNOCENT PEOPLE OUT OF HERE AS WE CAN--
--MAKE SURE THEY CAN'T TAKE HOSTAGES.
YOU DON'T KNOW WHAT YOU'RE TALKING ABOUT.

THIS ISN'T SOME POLITICAL THING... ALL THEY WANT IS YOU AND ME!
WE SHOW OURSELVES, THEY'LL FOLLOW US ANYWHERE.
SIMPLE AS THAT.

LET'S GO!

SO YOU'RE HANK'S NEW PARTNER, HUH? WHAT'S THE NAME? DOVE?
FUNNY. YOU REMIND ME OF SOMEONE ELSE. SOMEONE I THOUGHT WAS MY FRIEND.
REN... I'M NOT HIS PARTNER-- NOT THE WAY YOU THINK.

REN, I CAN'T EXPLAIN RIGHT NOW. JUST TRUST ME, YOU DON'T UNDERSTAND.
BUT YOU'RE TRYING.
DON'T SAY ANYTHING RASH THAT YOU-- OR I-- WILL REGRET LATER.

NO PROMISES, DOVE.
ALL'S FAIR...

CHOOM
WHERE'S THIS HAWK GUY?
YEAH, WE'RE GONNA RUN OUTTA TARGETS BEFORE HE SHOWS UP!
CHOOM

HERE I AM, BOYS-- BEHIND DOOR NUMBER TWO!
KRAKUNCH

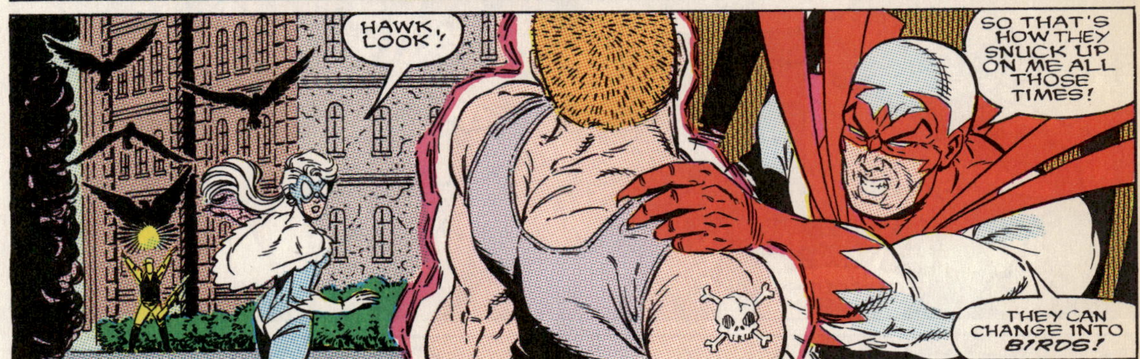
HAWK, LOOK!
SO THAT'S HOW THEY SNUCK UP ON ME ALL THOSE TIMES!
THEY CAN CHANGE INTO BIRDS!

HOLD ON, BUDDY-- YOU'RE GROUNDED!
CAN'T FLY AWAY WITHOUT THIS-- CAN YOU?

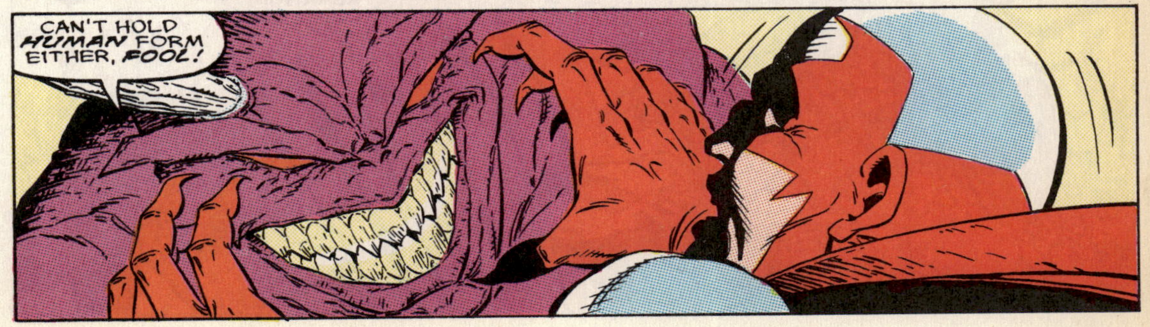
CAN'T HOLD HUMAN FORM EITHER, FOOL!

HOLY --!
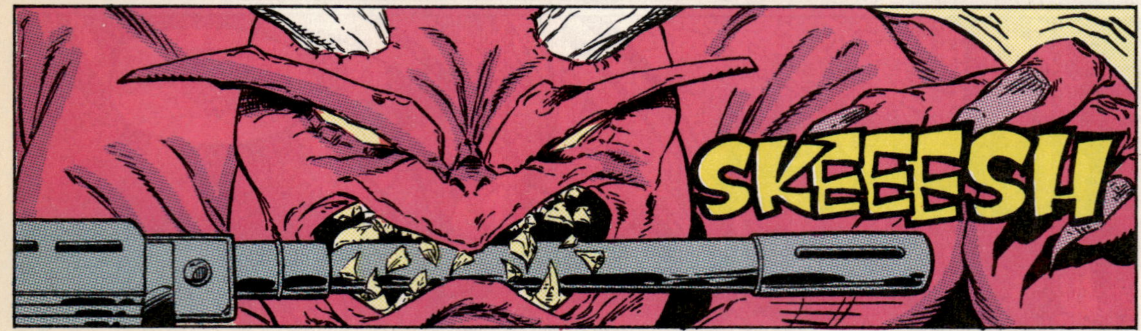
SKEEESH

I KNEW WHAT I WAS DOING. I HAD THE SITUATION UNDER CONTROL!
OF COURSE YOU DID.
HEADS UP-- INCOMING!

HOW MANY OF THESE CREATURES ARE THERE?
SILLY ME--I FORGOT TO CALL THE DEMONIC TERRORISTS HOTLINE THIS MORNING TO FIND OUT!

WATCH YER REAR, KID!

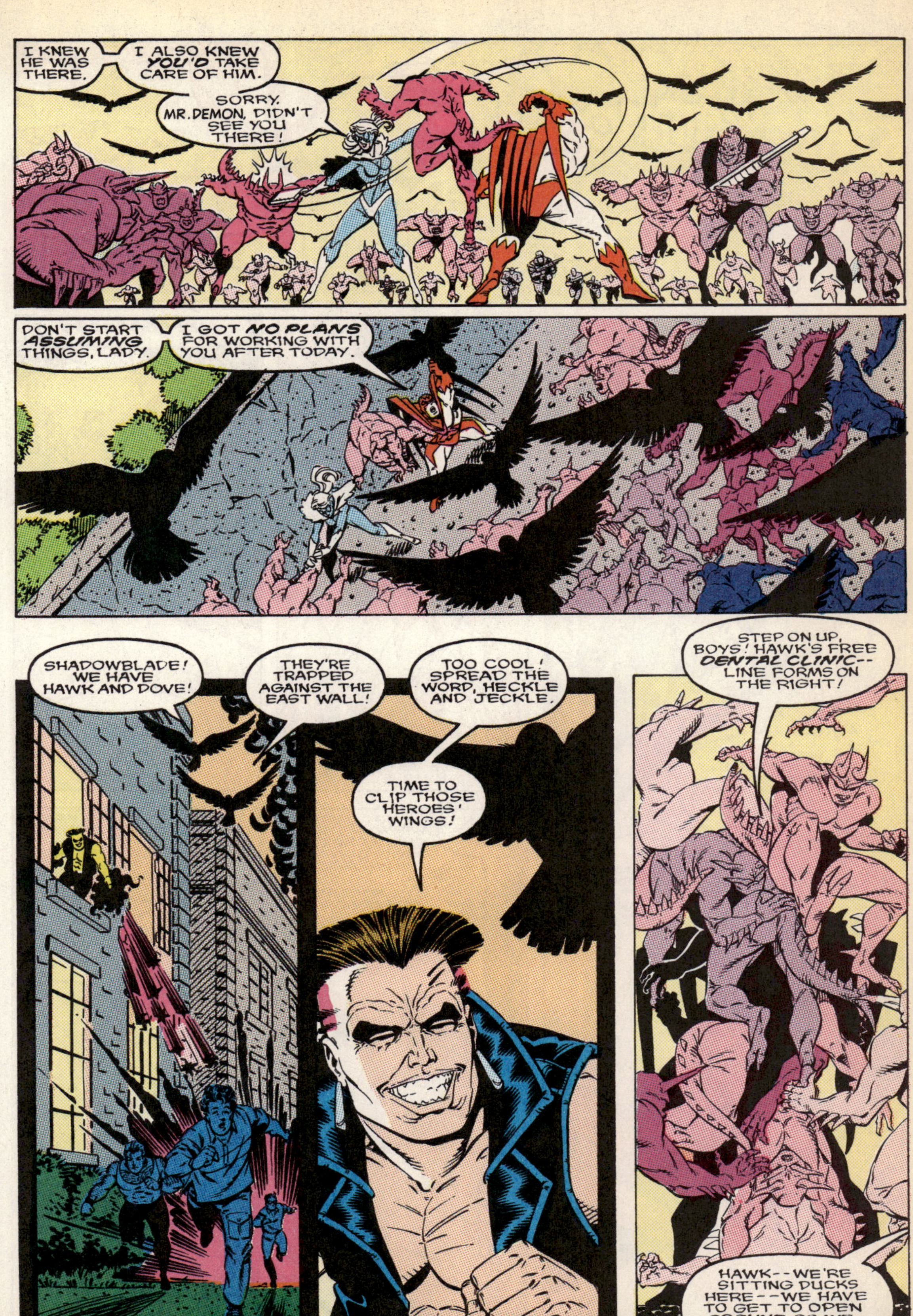
I KNEW HE WAS THERE.
I ALSO KNEW YOU'D TAKE CARE OF HIM.
SORRY, MR. DEMON, DIDN'T SEE YOU THERE!
DON'T START ASSUMING THINGS, LADY.
I GOT NO PLANS FOR WORKING WITH YOU AFTER TODAY.
SHADOWBLADE! WE HAVE HAWK AND DOVE!
THEY'RE TRAPPED AGAINST THE EAST WALL!
TOO COOL! SPREAD THE WORD, HECKLE AND JECKLE.
TIME TO CLIP THOSE HEROES' WINGS!
STEP ON UP, BOYS! HAWK'S FREE DENTAL CLINIC-- LINE FORMS ON THE RIGHT!
HAWK--WE'RE SITTING DUCKS HERE--WE HAVE TO GET TO OPEN GROUND SO WE CAN MANEUVER!

KATHOOM
BOOM

WELL, IF IT AIN'T MY OL' PAL, HAWK! KINDA FIGURED THIS WAS A PARTY IN YOUR HONOR.
HAUL IT UP HERE, SON, AND BRING YOUR PARTNER. WOULDN'T WANT YOU CAUGHT IN THE LINE OF FIRE, NOW, WOULD WE?

I'M DOIN' JUST FINE, WOLFSON! SO WHY DON'T YOU AND YOUR BOYS GO...
HAWK! HE COULD PROBABLY HELP END THIS A LOT FASTER!
I'M NOT WORKING WITH HIM, AND NO ONE CAN MAKE...

...MEEEEEEEEEE!
NICE MOVE, LADY. HOPE YOU LIVE TO TELL ABOUT IT.

I CAN HANDLE HIM.
NOT JUST HAWK-- THOSE THINGS AFTER YOU, THEY'RE COMING BACK!
EVERYONE-- POSITIONS!

THAT'S THE LAST STRAW! I'M GONNA--
HELLO, HAWK. I'M CAPTAIN ARSALA-- CALL ME SAL-- HEAD OF THE WASHINGTON SPECIAL CRIMES UNIT.
THIS YOUR PARTNER, DOVE? GOOD. WE NEED YOUR HELP.

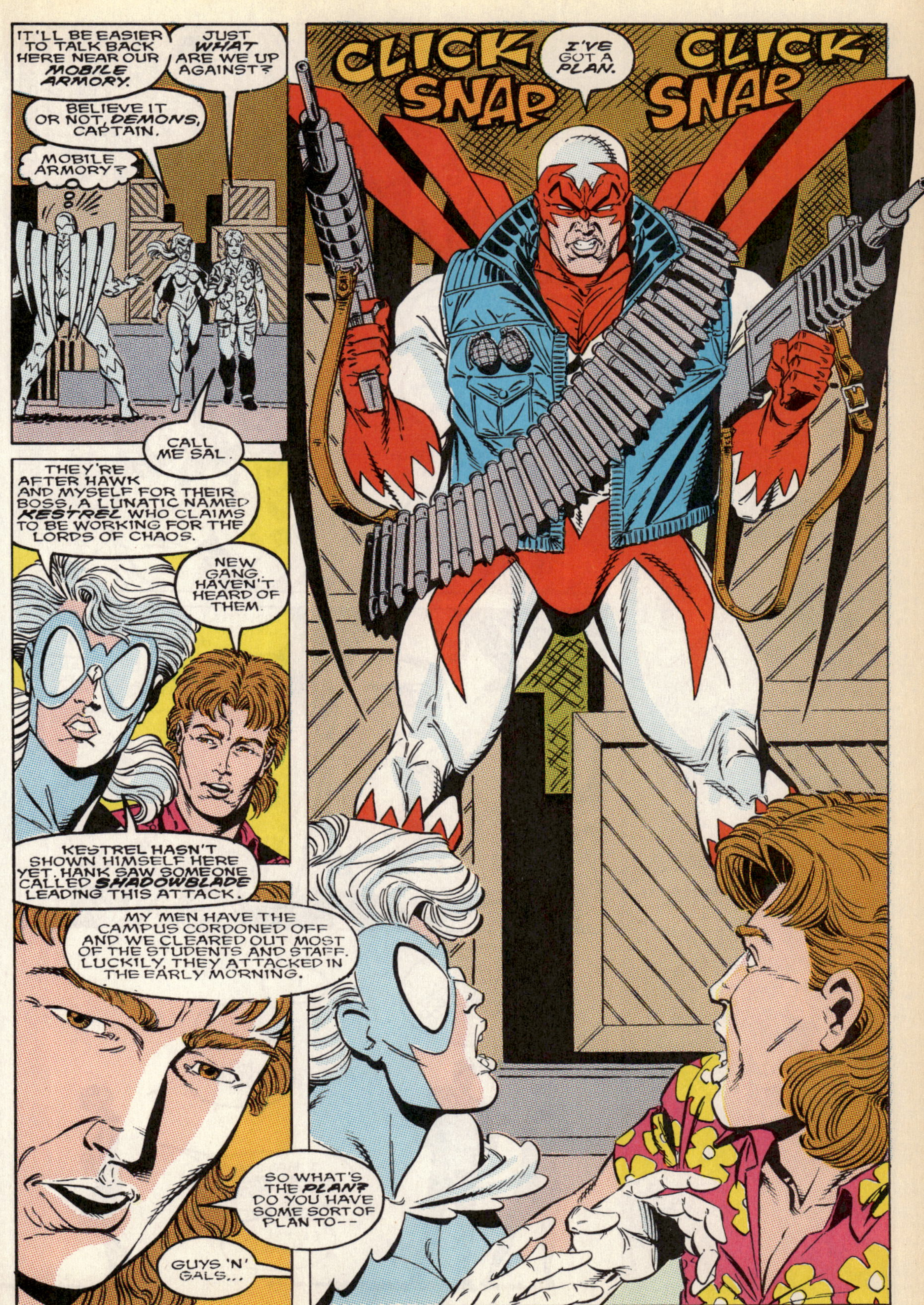
IT'LL BE EASIER TO TALK BACK HERE NEAR OUR MOBILE ARMORY.
JUST WHAT ARE WE UP AGAINST?
BELIEVE IT OR NOT, DEMONS, CAPTAIN.
MOBILE ARMORY?
CALL ME SAL.
THEY'RE AFTER HAWK AND MYSELF FOR THEIR BOSS, A LUNATIC NAMED KESTREL WHO CLAIMS TO BE WORKING FOR THE LORDS OF CHAOS.
NEW GANG. HAVEN'T HEARD OF THEM.
KESTREL HASN'T SHOWN HIMSELF HERE YET. HANK SAW SOMEONE CALLED SHADOWBLADE LEADING THIS ATTACK.
MY MEN HAVE THE CAMPUS CORDONED OFF AND WE CLEARED OUT MOST OF THE STUDENTS AND STAFF. LUCKILY, THEY ATTACKED IN THE EARLY MORNING.
SO WHAT'S THE PLAN? DO YOU HAVE SOME SORT OF PLAN TO--
GUYS 'N' GALS...
CLICK SNAP
I'VE GOT A PLAN.
CLICK SNAP

COLOR: IT'S ABOUT NOON NOW — CLOUDS MIX W/SMOKE FROM

THOSE WEAPONS ARE *STRICTLY* CITY-ISSUED. MY MEN HAVE BEEN *SPECIALLY* TRAINED...
ISN'T A GUN IN THE WORLD I DON'T KNOW HOW TO USE... "SAL".

NOW, YOU GONNA TRY TO STOP ME?
OR CAN I GET TO WORK?

NEVER MIND. LOOKS LIKE THE CHOICE'S BEEN MADE.
GLAD THESE THINGS AREN'T *HUMAN*. GIVES ME AN EXTRA *OPTION*.
BRAKKA
BRAKKA
BRAKKA
BRAKKA
YOUR RIGHT FLANK'S ABOUT TO BE RIPPED APART. RADIO 'EM THE CAVALRY'S ON ITS WAY.
YOU TWO CAN JOIN ME IF YOU'RE UP TO IT.
DISSOLVING DEMONS

I JUST WISH HE WAS A LITTLE *MORE CONFIDENT*. THAT'S ALL.
YOU NEED A WEAPON?
I'VE ALREADY GOT EVERYTHING I NEED.
I'LL SAY.

YEAH. BUDGET CUTS MADE US GET RID OF THE PIT BULLS--
WHAT IS IT? DO I HAVE TO COVER EVERYONE'S REAR TODAY?
--SO WE HAD TO SETTLE FOR YOU.
I KNOW YOU'RE NOT AS SMART, BUT YOU ARE UGLIER!
HARDY HAR HAR, PILLOW BOY.
COLOR: DEMONS DISSOLVE AFTER BEING "KILLED"
LOOK, WOLFIE, THIS IS A GOOD TIME AND ALL, BUT I MUSTA SHOT OR PUNCHED OR KICKED A HUNDRED DEMONS TODAY!
IT'S GETTING KINDA MONOTONOUS!
DON'T TELL ME--YOU GOT A CRAZY IDEA TO END THIS, RIGHT?
DEPENDS. YOU CALL STRAPPING A SHORT-FUSE BOMB ON MY CHEST AND BEIN' LIVE DEMON-BAIT CRAZY?
THAT AIN'T CRAZY, HOTSHOT--
--THAT'S THE ANSWER TO MY PRAYERS!

HAWK'S ATTACK IS ATTRACTING MOST OF THE DEMONS. IT'LL GIVE US A CHANCE TO CIRCLE AROUND.
Y'KNOW, FOR A BLOODBATH, I CERTAINLY DON'T SEE MANY BODIES.

THE DEMONS SEEM TO... DISSOLVE ONCE THEY'RE "KILLED". I'M NOT SURE IF THAT MEANS THEY'RE REALLY DEAD OR...
WHA--?

LOOK OUT!
POOM
POOM
THUNK
AAAAARGH!

ARE YOU ALL RIGHT?
WHOLE ARM'S NUMB.
WHAT WAS THAT?

DON'T TELL ME... SHADOWBLADE, RIGHT?
NICE TO SEE YOU REMEMBER YOUR OLD FRIENDS, DOVE.

I REALLY DON'T BELIEVE I'VE HAD THE HONOR, SIR.
OR MAYBE I DID, BUT IT JUST WASN'T AN HONOR.
YOU FREAKIN' SUPER-HEROES THINK YOU'RE SO HOT!
WELL, I CAN PLAY TOO, NOW.
THIS AIN'T NO STREET PUNK YOU'RE FACING NO MORE!
YOU'RE FROM THAT GANG IN THE PARK, AREN'T YOU? THE KID WITH THE SHURIKENS?
ONLY YOU'RE SO MUCH OLDER... AND YOUR POWERS...
MADE A DEAL WITH THE DEVIL, BABE.
JUST LIKE YOU DID TO GET YOUR FANCY OUTFIT.

I'M RUNNING SCARED! THERE'S TOO MANY OF YOU!
DEAR ME! THINK I'LL HIDE IN THE LIBRARY! I'LL BE SAFER THERE!

DAMN IF THE HOTSHOT WASN'T RIGHT! THOSE THINGS ARE AFTER HIM LIKE FLIES TO HONEY!
HOW LONG'S HE GOT LEFT?
48 SECONDS.

OH, NO--I'M TRAPPED.
HEEBIE JEEBIES...THERE'S NO PLACE LEFT TO RUN!
THEY'RE EATIN' IT UP! DIDN'T REALIZE WHAT A GOOD ACTOR I WAS!
I'LL JUST STRING 'EM ALONG--IT'S GOTTA BE MORE THAN A MINUTE BEFORE THIS BOX BLOWS!

TWELVE SECONDS...

...EIGHT...
C'MON, HOTSHOT. DON'T SCREW UP THIS TIME.
...SIX...

"...FIVE..."
KE-RASHH!

HIT IT, MEN!
COVER EVERY OPENING!
DON'T LET ANY OF THOSE THINGS OUT!

KA-THOOM

SAY! SHE BLOWED UP REAL GOOD!
BY THE WAY, WOLFIE, THANKS FOR THE TEN-SECOND WARNING BEEPER.
NOT THAT YOU NEEDED IT.
NOT THAT I NEEDED IT.

WHY DON'T YOU JUST LIE DOWN AND DIE, DOVE?
HERE, I'LL HELP!

YOU KNOW I'M GOING TO TRASH YOU 'CAUSE I AM SUPREME --

KA-THOOM
SOUNDS LIKE MY PALS GOT HAWK.
WAIT'LL THE BOSS SEES HOW EASILY WE KICKED BOTH YOUR--

SPLOOSH
--!ARGRPH!
WATCH THE LANGUAGE, SHADOWBLADE.

OR I'LL HAVE TO WASH YOUR MOUTH OUT AGAIN!
CAPTAIN, I'LL GET SOME HELP FOR YOU AS SOON AS I FINISH WITH MR. NINJA HERE.
THREE MINUTES TOPS.

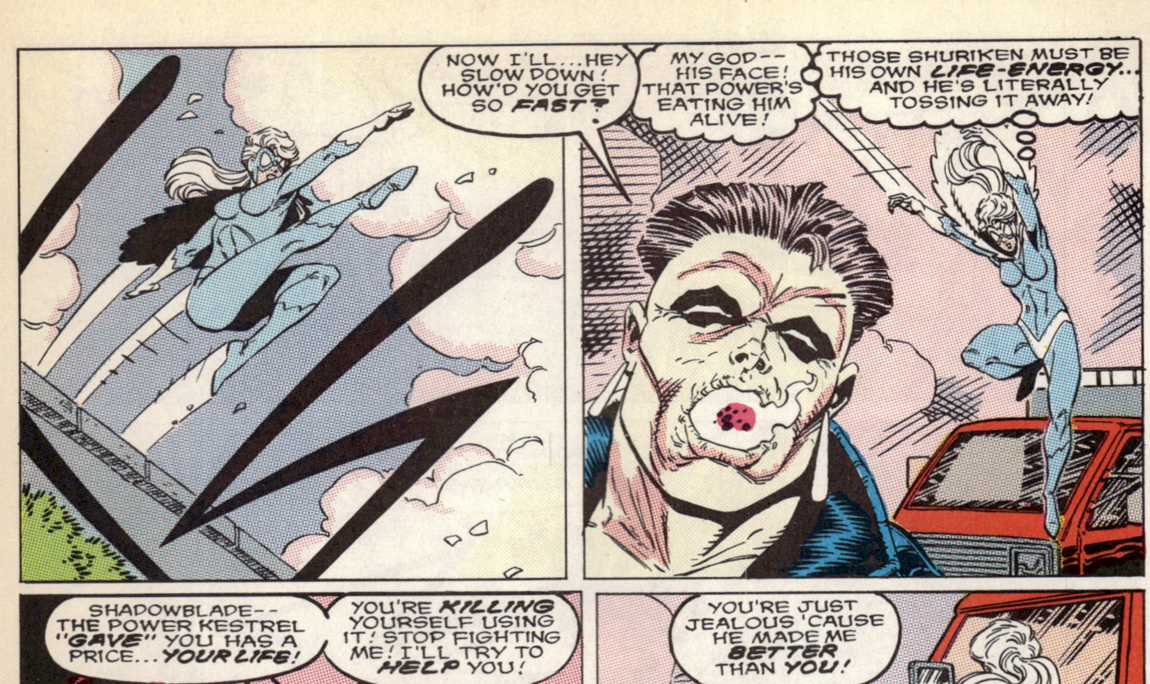
NOW I'LL... HEY SLOW DOWN! HOW'D YOU GET SO FAST?
MY GOD-- HIS FACE! THAT POWER'S EATING HIM ALIVE!
THOSE SHURIKEN MUST BE HIS OWN LIFE-ENERGY... AND HE'S LITERALLY TOSSING IT AWAY!

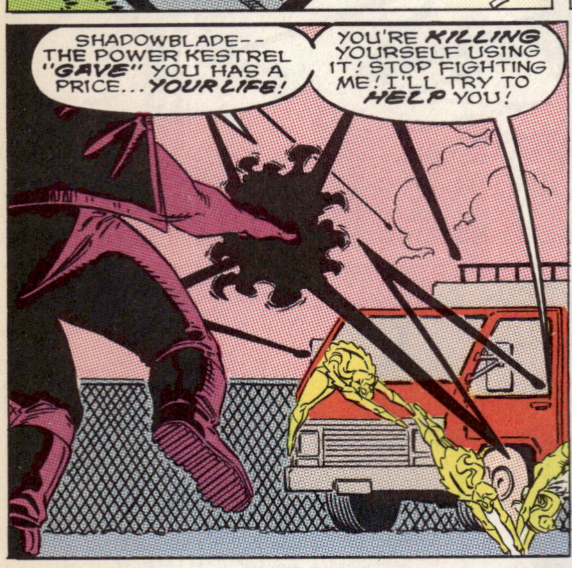
SHADOWBLADE-- THE POWER KESTREL "GAVE" YOU HAS A PRICE... YOUR LIFE!
YOU'RE KILLING YOURSELF USING IT! STOP FIGHTING ME! I'LL TRY TO HELP YOU!

YOU'RE JUST JEALOUS 'CAUSE HE MADE ME BETTER THAN YOU!
I'M NOT GONNA FALL FOR ANY OF YOUR OLD...

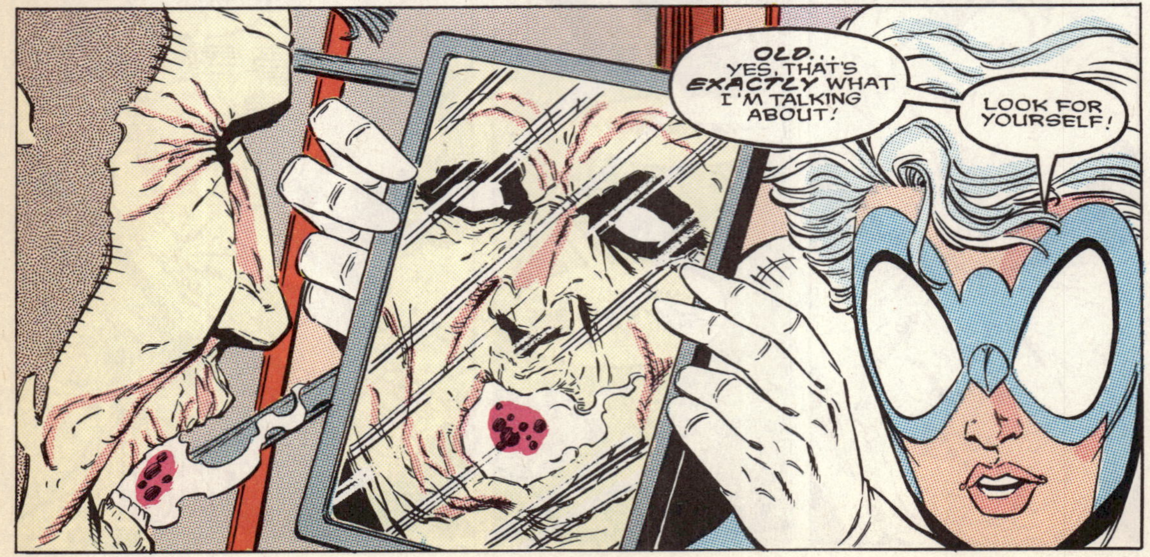
OLD... YES, THAT'S EXACTLY WHAT I'M TALKING ABOUT!
LOOK FOR YOURSELF!

AAAAAH!
WHAT DID YOU DO TO ME, WITCH?
IT'S NOT ME. IT'S KESTREL.

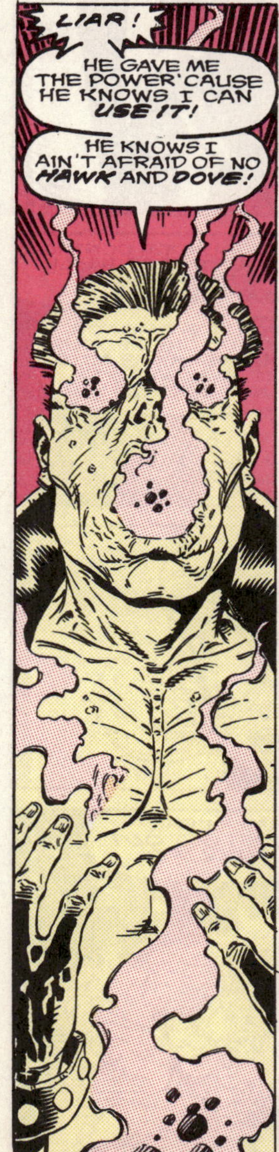
LIAR!
HE GAVE ME THE POWER 'CAUSE HE KNOWS I CAN USE IT!
HE KNOWS I AIN'T AFRAID OF NO HAWK AND DOVE!

EXACTLY. AND HE USED THAT ANGER TO MAKE YOU HIS WEAPON.
SHUT UP! THIS IS MY BIG CHANCE!

I CAN BEAT YOU! I CAN SHOW EVERYONE THAT I AIN'T JUSTA...

...KID...

THERE YOU ARE. THOUGHT YOU MIGHT NEED SOME HELP WITH THAT SHADOWBLADE GOON.
BUT IT LOOKS LIKE HE'S ALL TAKEN CARE OF.
YEAH?
TAKEN CARE OF.

EXCUSE ME. I HAVE TO GET SOME HELP FOR CAPTAIN ARSALA. HE WAS HURT...
WOLFSON'S MEN ALREADY GOT HIM.
HE'LL BE ALL RIGHT. HAS TO, IF HE WANTS TO STAY IN THIS LINE OF WORK.

EVERYTHING'S UNDER CONTROL HERE. DANGER'S PAST. WE'LL BE CHANGING BACK TO NORMAL SOON.
GUESS IT'S TIME FOR YOU TO DO ONE OF YOUR DISAPPEARING ACTS. SLIP AWAY WHILE I'M NOT LOOKIN'.

NOT THIS TIME, HAWK.
I DON'T WANT WHAT HAPPENED WITH REN TO HAPPEN TO ANYONE ELSE.
IT'S TIME FOR YOU TO LEARN WHO I REALLY AM.
IT'S TIME TO BE HONEST.

I'M NOT INTERESTED, LADY.
WE HAD A DEAL-- NOW JUST GET OUT OF MY LIFE.

AND WHAT ABOUT KESTREL? HE'S STILL OUT THERE. HE ALMOST KILLED YOU ONCE ALREADY!
I CAN TAKE CARE OF MYSELF.

AND IF YOU NEED HELP? WHO WILL YOU GRAB OFF THE STREETS THEN?
WHO WILL YOU THINK IS DOVE NEXT TIME?

MAYBE I ALREADY KNOW.
MAYBE I THOUGHT-- WHO DO I KNOW WHO'S ATHLETIC?
WHO'S BOSSY?
WHO'S ALWAYS BEEN ON MY CASE?

OKAY, I WAS WRONG ABOUT REN. ANYONE CAN MAKE A MISTAKE ONCE.
SHOULD HAVE KNOWN RIGHT OFF IT WAS YOU--
--DONNA!
WELL, YOU'RE GETTING WARMER.

DAWN?
BUT HOW...? WHEN DID...?
I KNEW YOU COULD GET IT IF YOU HAD THREE GUESSES.

I'LL ANSWER ANY QUESTIONS, BUT ONLY IF WE CAN MAKE A DEAL.
I WANT TO GET KESTREL. LET ME HELP STOP HIM FROM KILLING AGAIN.
...OKAY, LADY. YOU'VE GOT A DEAL.

DC
HAWK & DOVE™
5
HOLIDAY
U.S. $1.00
CAN $1.35
APPROVED BY THE COMICS CODE AUTHORITY
FIVE ISSUE MINI-SERIES
BY KESEL, LIEFELD & KESEL
FROM THE CHAOS AN ENDING!
LIEFELD
KESEL

"I REMEMBER EVERYTHING SO CLEARLY...
"MY MOTHER WAS IN LONDON ON BUSINESS--SHE'S A DIPLOMATIC COURIER. I WAS ATTENDING OXFORD..."
"WHEN *WAS* THIS?"

"REMEMBER THE TIME WHEN ALL THE SKIES TURNED *RED?*"
"OH, YEAH, *THEN*. WHEN DOVE..."
"YES. LONDON WAS A MADHOUSE. EVERYONE THOUGHT IT WAS THE END OF THE WORLD.
"TERRORISTS TOOK OVER THE AMERICAN EMBASSY. ONE OF THE HOSTAGES WAS MY MOTHER.
G-4246

LIVE
"IT WAS SOME RADICAL TERRORIST GROUP. THEY RANTED ON ABOUT HOW THE RED SKIES HAD SOMETHING TO DO WITH *RUSSIA* AND MAGGIE THATCHER'S SECRET *DRUG CARTEL*...
"THEY DIDN'T EVEN MAKE ANY DEMANDS. EVERYTHING HAD JUST SLIPPED INTO *CHAOS*.
UNIDENTIFIED TERRORIST AND AMERICAN HOSTAGE MARIE GRANGER

"WASHINGTON AND WHITEHALL WERE HELPLESS. ALL THEIR ARMIES, POLICE AND SPECIAL FORCES WERE ON THE STREETS TRYING TO CONTROL THE PANIC.
"AND THEN THE TERRORISTS ANNOUNCED THEY WOULD BLOW UP THE EMBASSY AT PRECISELY 9:11 THAT NIGHT.
"I DIDN'T KNOW WHERE TO TURN. THEY WERE GOING TO BLOW UP MY *MOM*, AND THERE WAS NOTHING I COULD DO!"
"DON'T TELL ME. THEN A MYSTERIOUS VOICE CAME OUTTA *NOWHERE* AND GAVE YOU SUPER-POWERS."

"THAT'S RIGHT, ONLY IT ALMOST SOUNDED LIKE MORE THAN ONE VOICE. A SHIMMERING *HARMONY*...
"IT OFFERED ME A CHANCE TO MAKE *ORDER* FROM THIS CHAOS. ALL I HAD TO DO WAS SAY THE WORD..."

HAWK & DOVE™
BLOOD BROTHERS
BARBARA AND KARL KESEL WRITERS
ROB LIEFELD PENCILLER
KARL KESEL INKER
JANICE CHIANG LETTERER
GLENN WHITMORE COLORIST
RENÉE WITTERSTAETTER ASSISTANT EDITOR
MIKE CARLIN EDITOR
DOVE!
"I REMEMBER HEARING BIG BEN CHIME THE FIRST TIME I BECAME DOVE. IT WAS NINE O'CLOCK.
"ELEVEN BIRDS WERE STARTLED INTO FLIGHT BY THE BELLS. I COULD COUNT THEM JUST BY THE SOUND OF THEIR WINGS.
"AND ELEVEN WAS THE NUMBER OF MINUTES I HAD LEFT BEFORE THE EMBASSY BLEW UP.

"IT'S HARD TO DESCRIBE WHAT HAPPENS WHEN I BECOME DOVE...
"I'VE ALWAYS BEEN A GOOD JUDGE OF PEOPLE, BUT AS DOVE-- IT'S LIKE I'M WORKING ON A SUPERNATURAL LEVEL.
"EACH GESTURE REVEALS A THOUSAND CLUES ABOUT A PERSON. IN SECONDS, I KNOW HOW EVERYONE IN A ROOM WILL ACT AND REACT..."

"LIKE WHAT THE VOICE TOLD ME-- WHAT I'M GOOD AT NORMALLY, I'M SUPER-GOOD AT AS HAWK!"
"EXACTLY, BUT IT'S NOT LIMITED TO PEOPLE. FOR INSTANCE, IF I SEE A CHAIR, I CAN SENSE ITS WEIGHT, ITS POTENTIAL...

"...I KNOW PRECISELY WHERE TO STRIKE IT TO MOST EFFECTIVELY TRIP UP MY ATTACKER.
"I CAN SENSE EXACTLY WHERE A GUN IS POINTED, FEEL WHEN IT IS ABOUT TO BE FIRED.
"EVERYTHING IS IN SHARP FOCUS. I ABSORB EVERY DETAIL AROUND ME."
"IT'S THE EXACT OPPOSITE FOR ME... I KINDA LOSE TRACK OF EVERYTHING EXCEPT WHAT I'M AIMIN' AT."

"YOU'RE A ZOOM LENS, I'M WIDE-ANGLE-- MY MIND TAKES IT ALL IN INSTANTLY, SORTING THROUGH ALL EVIDENCE TO FIND PATTERNS AND POSSIBILITIES.
"I'M IN CONTROL, READY FOR ANYTHING.

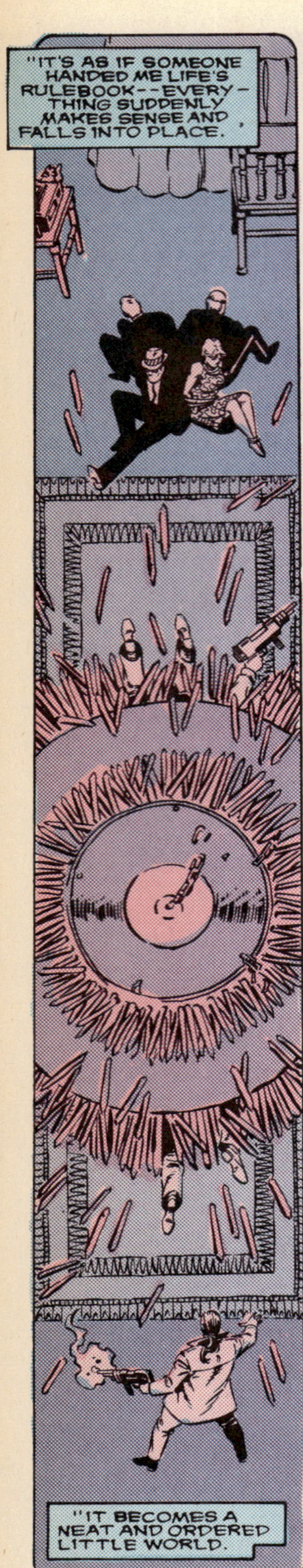

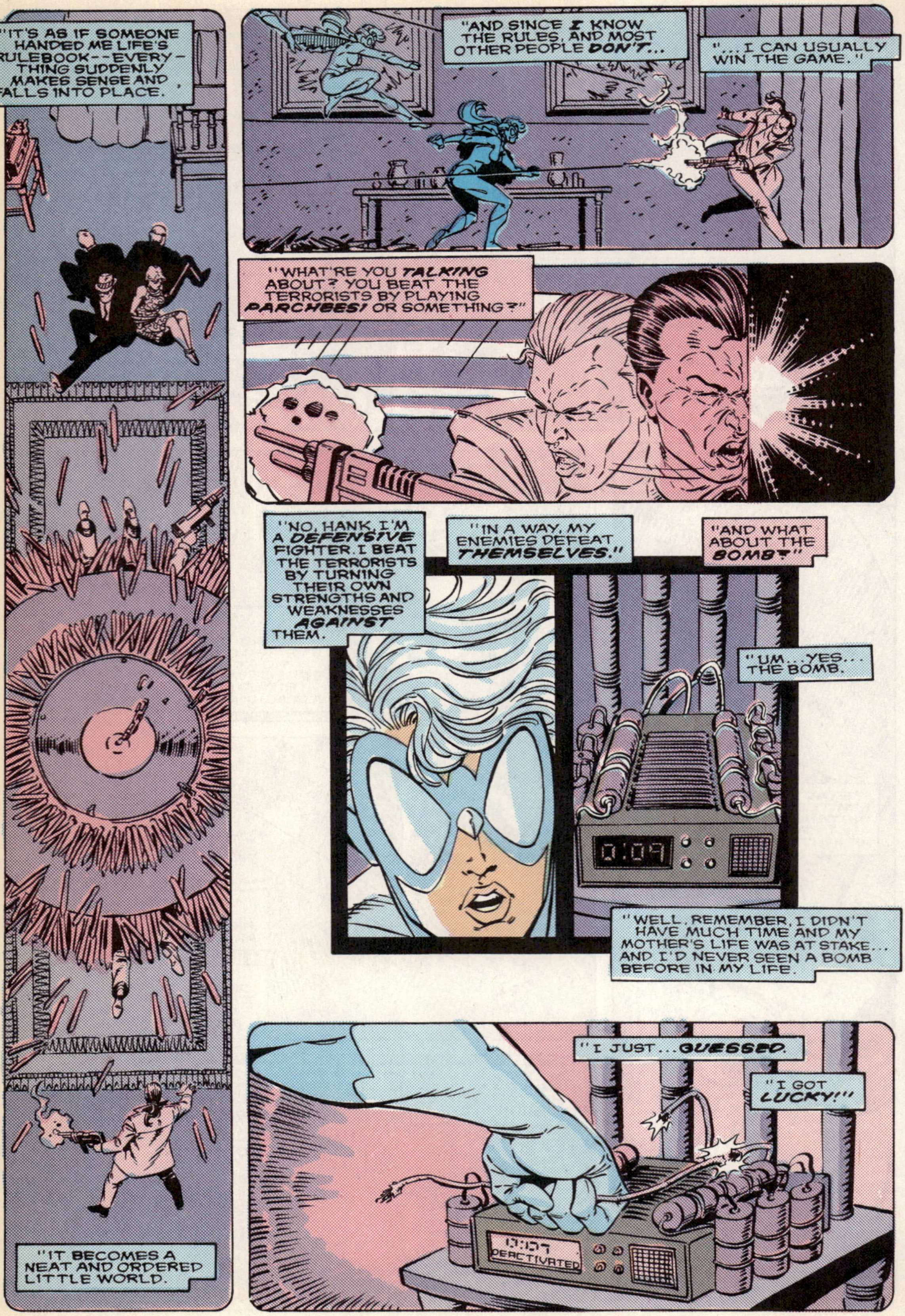

"AND SINCE *I* KNOW THE RULES, AND MOST OTHER PEOPLE *DON'T*...

"...I CAN USUALLY WIN THE GAME."

"WHAT'RE YOU *TALKING* ABOUT? YOU BEAT THE TERRORISTS BY PLAYING *PARCHEESI* OR SOMETHING?"

"NO, HANK, I'M A *DEFENSIVE* FIGHTER. I BEAT THE TERRORISTS BY TURNING THEIR OWN STRENGTHS AND WEAKNESSES *AGAINST* THEM.

"IN A WAY, MY ENEMIES DEFEAT *THEMSELVES*."

"AND WHAT ABOUT THE *BOMB*?"

"UM... YES... THE BOMB.

0:09

"WELL, REMEMBER, I DIDN'T HAVE MUCH TIME AND MY MOTHER'S LIFE WAS AT STAKE... AND I'D NEVER SEEN A BOMB BEFORE IN MY LIFE.

"YOU GUESSED?!"
"HEY, I'M A FOREIGN RELATIONS MAJOR, NOT A SPY. FOR SOME STRANGE REASON, I NEVER STUDIED HOW TO DEFUSE A BOMB!"

"SO AFTER ALL THE DANGER WAS OVER, YOU CHANGED BACK TO DAWN GRANGER, RIGHT?"
"YES. FOR POLITICAL REASONS, THE WHOLE AFFAIR WAS DOWN-PLAYED. DOVE WAS NEVER MENTIONED ANYWHERE."

THAT WHEN YOU STARTED FOLLOWING ME?
NO, I FIRST HEARD THAT DOVE WAS DEAD, THEN...
...LOOK, I'M REALLY THIRSTY. DO YOU HAVE ANYTHING TO DRINK?

SURE, GOT SOME FLAT JOLT, SOME GATORADE, AND SOME MILK.
WHOOPS. STRIKE THE MILK.
I'LL TAKE WATER.

SEE, I THOUGHT I WAS JUST ANOTHER DOVE--LIKE ALL THOSE GREEN LANTERNS.
WHEN I FOUND OUT ABOUT YOUR DOVE...
I KNEW I WAS THE ONLY ONE.
I KNEW I HAD TO FIND YOU.

I SOON DISCOVERED THAT WHEREVER HAWK WAS SEEN, HANK HALL WASN'T FAR AWAY.
YOU SURE LIKE TRAVELODGES, DON'T YOU?
IT'S THAT SLEEPWALKING BEAR-- HE'S GREAT!

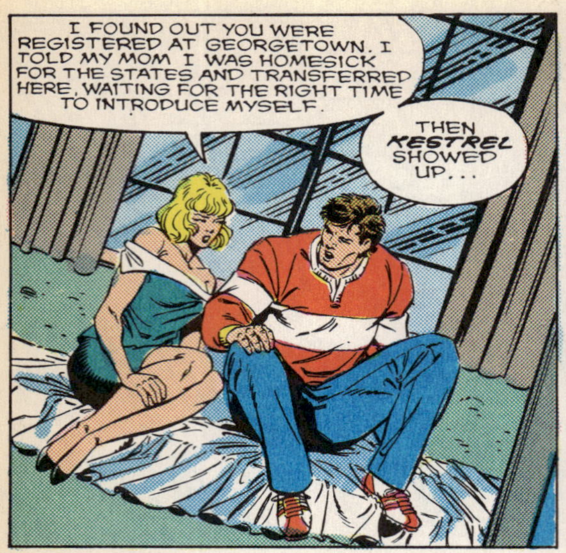
I FOUND OUT YOU WERE REGISTERED AT GEORGETOWN. I TOLD MY MOM I WAS HOMESICK FOR THE STATES AND TRANSFERRED HERE, WAITING FOR THE RIGHT TIME TO INTRODUCE MYSELF.
THEN KESTREL SHOWED UP...

MAYBE I SHOULD HAVE WAITED, BUT I FELT THAT WE BELONGED TOGETHER.
WELL, THIS IS COZY!
EVENING, SON!

MOM! DAD! HI!
WHAT'RE YOU DOING HERE?
AFTER THAT ATTACK ON THE CAMPUS, WE WANTED TO MAKE SURE YOU WERE ALL RIGHT.
WE COULDN'T REACH YOU BY PHONE, AND YOU DID GIVE US A COPY KEY...

WELL... I UNPLUGGED THE PHONE SO...
YOU DON'T HAVE TO EXPLAIN, DEAR. YOU'RE AN ADULT. HOPEFULLY A CAUTIOUS ADULT.
THIS MILK IS BAD-- YOU SHOULD THROW IT OUT.
MOM! IT'S NOT WHAT YOU'RE THINKING! WE--

WE'LL LET OURSELVES OUT, DEAR. DON'T FORGET DINNER TOMORROW.
AND WHY DON'T YOU BRING YOUR FRIEND? BYE, NOW.
NICE TO SEE HIM TAKING AN INTEREST IN GIRLS AGAIN.

UM... THOSE WERE MY PARENTS...
I'D FIGURED THAT ONE OUT.

CRASH
WASN'T THAT CHARMING!
IT'S ONE OF KESTREL'S GOONS!
HA--!

WAIT, HANK--THIS ISN'T AN ATTACK... NOT WITH ONLY ONE OF THEM...
I THINK HE'S JUST A MESSENGER.

THAT'S RIGHT.
KESTREL'S SORRY HE COULDN'T MAKE IT TO THE CAMPUS EARLIER.
THOUGHT MAYBE YOU TWO COULD JOIN HIM AT THE USUAL PLACE. SAY, IN ABOUT FIFTEEN MINUTES.
IF NOT, HE MIGHT HAVE TO VISIT THAT SWEET OLD COUPLE WHO WERE JUST HERE.

AND HE'LL BE ABLE TO FIND THEM NOW THAT HE KNOWS YOUR NAME, HAWK--
OR SHOULD I SAY, HANK HALL!
FIFTEEN MINUTES!

LET HIM GO, HANK. WE'VE GOT TO THINK...
LET HIM GO?
HE JUST THREATENED MY FOLKS! IF DON WERE HERE, HE WOULDN'T--

TAKE A CLOSE LOOK, HANK--I MAY BE YOUR PARTNER, BUT I'M NOT YOUR BROTHER!
LADY, YOU AIN'T EVEN MY PARTNER.
LET'S GO--IT'S GONNA TAKE ALL OUR TIME TO GET TO THE "USUAL PLACE"...

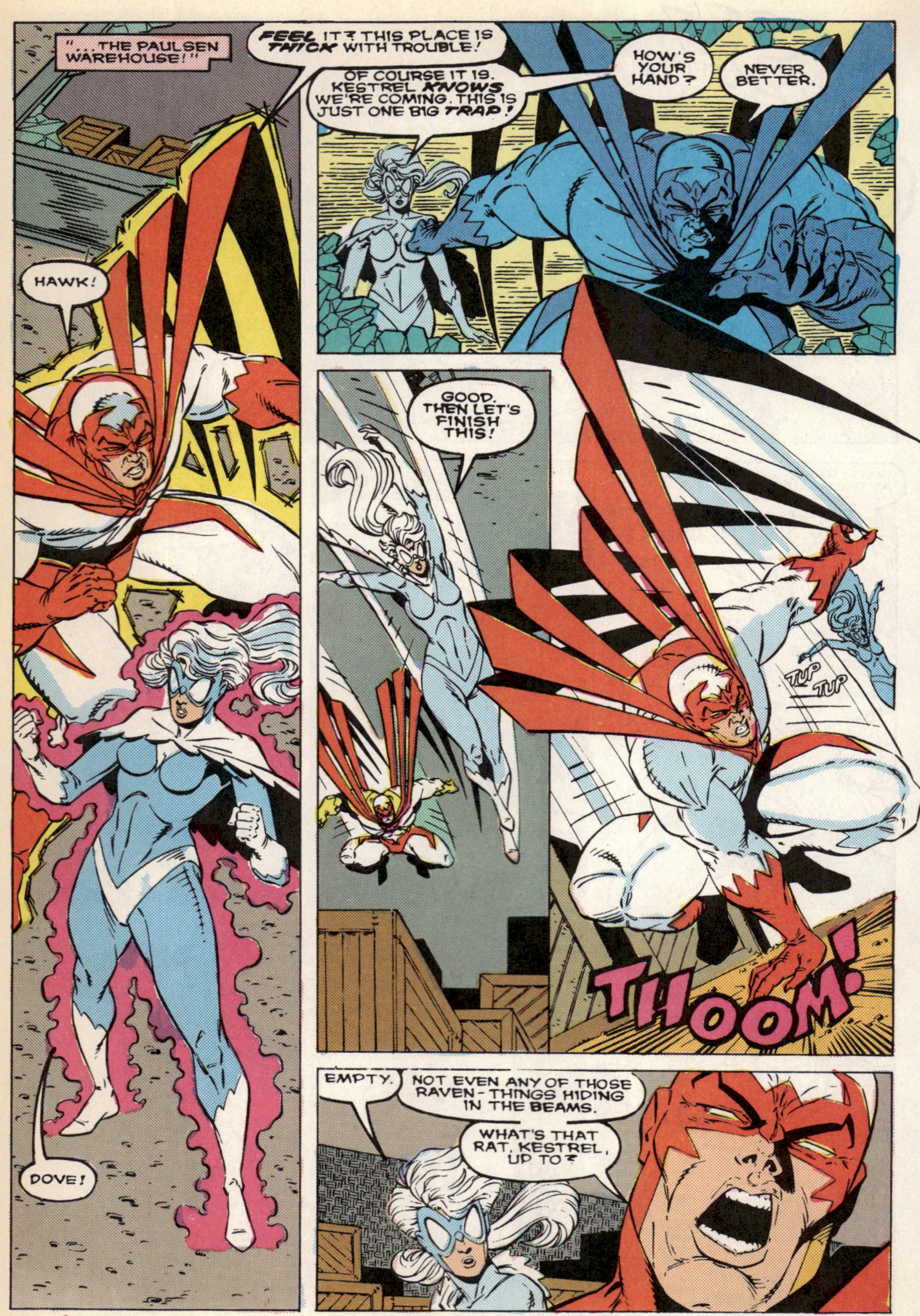
"...THE PAULSEN WAREHOUSE!"
FEEL IT? THIS PLACE IS THICK WITH TROUBLE!
OF COURSE IT IS. KESTREL KNOWS WE'RE COMING. THIS IS JUST ONE BIG TRAP!
HOW'S YOUR HAND?
NEVER BETTER.
HAWK!
DOVE!
GOOD. THEN LET'S FINISH THIS!
TUP TUP
THOOM!
EMPTY.
NOT EVEN ANY OF THOSE RAVEN-THINGS HIDING IN THE BEAMS.
WHAT'S THAT RAT, KESTREL, UP TO?

HMMM. WHAT DO WE HAVE HERE? NEVER NOTICED THIS DOOR BEFORE.
WHAT DOOR?
YOU GOT NO EYES? THE DOOR I'M ABOUT TO OPEN.
HAWK-- ALL I SEE IS EMPTY WALL.
THEN THIS MUST BE WHERE WE GOTTA GO!
OPEN--
CAREFUL, HAWK. WE DON'T KNOW--
--SESAME!
--WHERE THIS SUPPOSED DOOR--
--GOES...!

HAWK! DOVE! SO NICE OF YOU TO COME!
KESTREL, YOU SLIMEBUCKET-- WHAT SORT OF SCREWBALL PLACE IS THIS?
DON'T YOU RECOGNIZE IT, HAWK? THIS IS WHERE YOUR POWER COMES FROM!
THIS IS THE CHAOS REALM!

WELCOME HOME, HAWK. I HOPE YOU'RE HERE TO STAY.
IN FACT, I INSIST!

WHAT THE--!

UNGHH!
DON'T KNOW WHAT'S WRONG WITH ME...
THIS PLACE IS SO CONFUSING... NOTHING MAKES SENSE.
IT'S SO HARD TO KEEP MY THOUGHTS STRAIGHT...

KESTREL, GET YOUR SLIMY FACE OVER HERE! I WANT YOU!

I'M GONNA PAY YOU BACK FOR ALL THE TROUBLE YOU'VE CAUSED ME, SICKO!
NOTHING'S GONNA STOP ME!
THESE THE BEST YOU'VE GOT, KESTREL? THEY'RE TOOTHPICKS!
YOU SCARED OF ME, CREEP? SCARED TO FIGHT ME ONE-TO-ONE?
YOU SHOULD BE, KESTREL--
--'CAUSE THERE'S HELL TO PAY!
EXCELLENT, HAWK--BY THE TIME MY MINIONS ARE DONE WITH YOU, YOU'LL BE IN THE PERFECT STATE OF MIND TO JOIN ME!
AND, SPEAKING OF PARTNERS...

EVERYTHING KEEPS SHIFTING AND CHANGING, LIKE I'M IN SOMEBODY'S FEVER DREAM...
DAMMIT, GIRL--PULL YOURSELF TOGETHER!
YOU HAVE TO HELP HAWK!

I DON'T THINK I'D WORRY ABOUT HAWK IF I WERE YOU...

YOU'RE A LITTLE SLOW TODAY, DOVE. SOMETHING WRONG?
A LITTLE DISORIENTED, PERHAPS? AN AGENT OF ORDER NOT LIKING THE RANDOM NATURE OF THE CHAOS REALM?

BUT WHAT DO I KNOW? YOU YOURSELF SAID I'M JUST A LUNATIC IN A COSTUME.
HOW... DO YOU KNOW... SO MUCH ABOUT US, KESTREL?
THE REAL QUESTION IS, DOVE...
...HOW DO YOU KNOW SO LITTLE?

IT'S ALL AN EXPERIMENT, DOVE!
YOU AND HAWK ARE JUST MICE IN A MAZE.
YOU RUN BACK AND FORTH UP AND DOWN, AROUND AND AROUND...
BUT YOU'LL NEVER KNOW WHY...
YOU'LL NEVER KNOW WHAT IT WAS ALL ABOUT, DOVE...
...BECAUSE YOUR MAZE JUST CAME TO A DEAD END!
SAY "CHEESE"!

IF I'D STAYED ON THAT ROCK ONE SECOND LONGER...
I'D BE DEAD.
EVEN KESTREL COULDN'T HAVE SURVIVED THAT!
PLEASE, GOD, KESTREL DIDN'T SURVIVE!
WORRIED ABOUT ME, DOVE? DON'T BE.

NOTHING CAN KILL ME!
YOU, ON THE OTHER HAND...

RUNNING OUT OF TRICKS, DOVE? THAT'S THE SAME WAY YOU DODGED ME BEFORE.
DIDN'T YOU THINK I'D REMEMBER, AND BE READY?

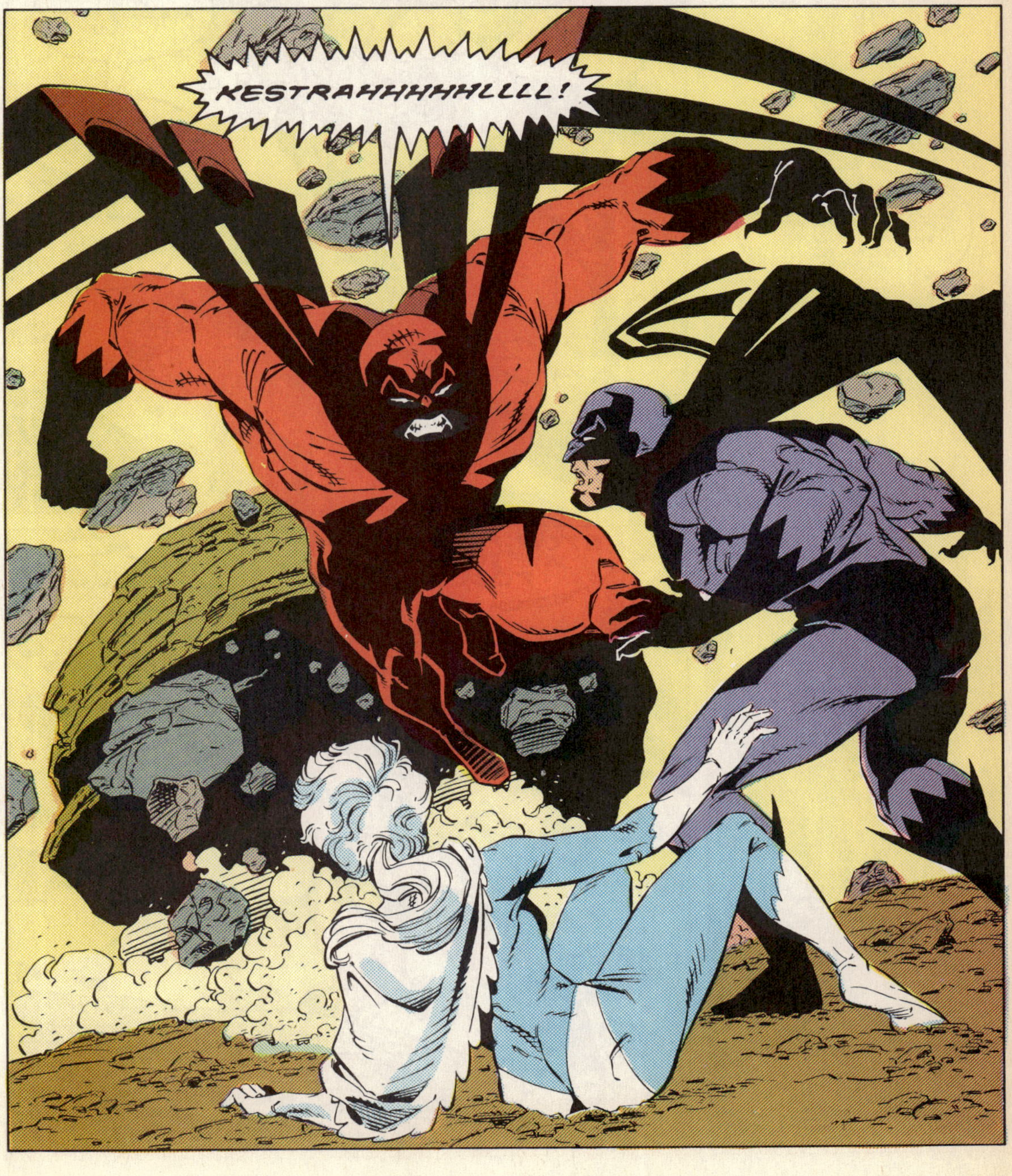

KESTRAHHHHHLLLLL!

IS THIS WHAT YOU WANT, HUH?
WANT ME TO SLAG YOUR FACE NOW? IS THAT WHAT YOU'RE LOOKING FOR?
HUH? WHAT?

I CAN'T HEAR YOU!
HAWK! WHAT HAPPENED TO YOU?
THIS PLACE IS AFFECTING US BOTH--
YOU'D BETTER--

STOP TELLIN' ME WHAT TO DO!
URGK!

YOU WANT TO BE MY PARTNER, LADY, BUT YOU TREAT ME LIKE HIRED HELP AND I'M SICK OF IT!
I KNOW WHAT I'M DOING AND YOU'D BETTER LEAVE ME ALONE OR ELSE I'LL--

DO IT, HAWK.
SHE DOESN'T UNDERSTAND YOU... NEVER WILL... NOT LIKE I DO.
SHE CONFUSES YOU, HAWK--MAKES YOU WEAK. GET RID OF HER.
JOIN ME, HAWK. WE WERE MEANT TO BE A TEAM. WE'RE SO ALIKE WE COULD BE MORE THAN PARTNERS...

...WE COULD BE BROTHERS...
...BLOOD BROTHERS!

NO.
NOT BROTHERS.
NOT WITH YOU.
NOT WITH ANYONE EVER AGAIN.
ALL RIGHT, DOVE...

ANY SUGGESTIONS HOW TO TAKE THIS SUCKER OUT...
...PARTNER?

YOU'VE FAILED, KESTREL!
YOW.
HAWK.
YOU KNOW THE PRICE OF FAILURE!
NO! I CAN STILL WIN HIM OVER! GIVE ME TIME...

WE HAVE TO GET OUT OF HERE!
MORE TIME...

YOU KNOW WHAT YOU'RE DOING, RIGHT?
NO! BUT WE CAN'T GO ANY PLACE WORSE THAN HERE!

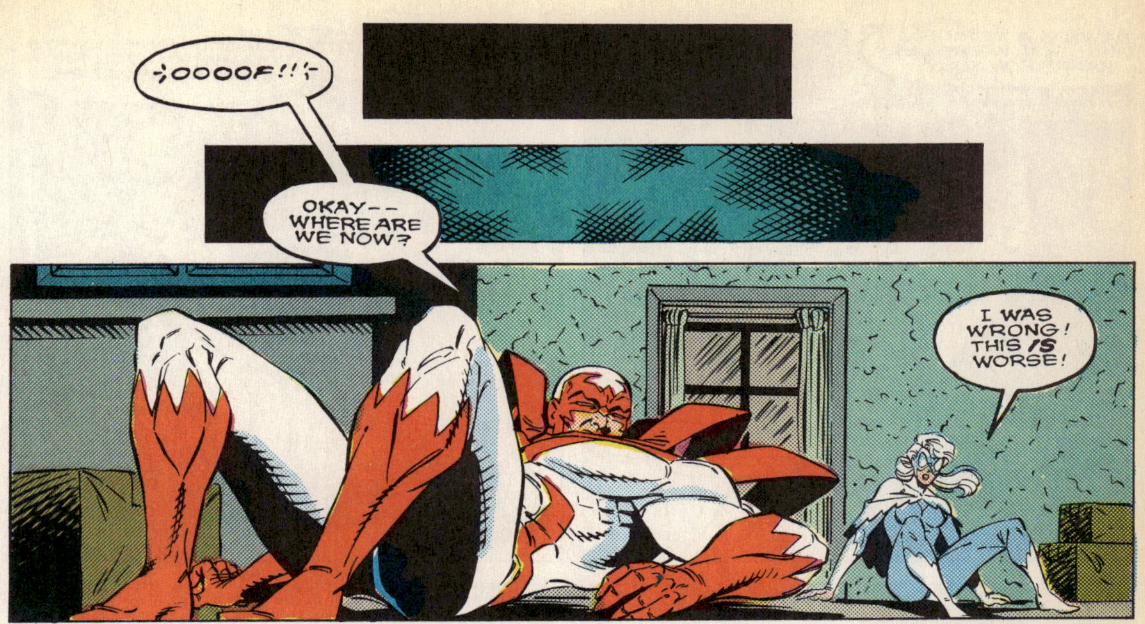

OOOOF!!
OKAY-- WHERE ARE WE NOW?
I WAS WRONG! THIS *IS* WORSE!

IT'S YOUR *APARTMENT*!
VERY FUNNY. A REGULAR LAUGH RIOT!
WHAT ABOUT *KESTREL?* WHAT HAPPENED TO HIM BACK THERE?

I DON'T KNOW, HAWK, I--
LOOK, WE'RE CHANGING BACK... THE DANGER'S *OVER*.
TELL YA WHAT I THINK, DAWN--
I THINK WE *KICKED HIS BUTT*.

I THINK YOU'RE RIGHT.
DAMN! IT'S GREAT TO BE ALIVE! C'MON, I'LL BUY YOU BREAKFAST...
...AN' WHAT'RE YOU DOING FOR *DINNER*?

A WONDERFUL SPINACH SOUFFLE, MRS. HALL. FROM THE CHEZ BIEN RECIPE, I ASSUME?
YOU *NOTICED?* I DO COOK A LOT OF FRENCH CUISINE. HANK WILL ACTUALLY *EAT* FRENCH FOODS...
...ESPECIALLY FRENCH FRIES...

DAWN'S A TERRIFIC GIRL, SON. WE'RE VERY HAPPY FOR YOU.
DAD--HOW MANY TIMES I GOTTA TELL YOU? WE'RE JUST FRIENDS. I THINK OF HER MORE LIKE A... SISTER.

THIS WAS TAKEN AT YELLOWSTONE...
DON AND HANK ALWAYS FOUGHT, BUT YOU KNOW SIBLING RIVALRY...
AND I KNOW HANK!

WHAT'S THIS?
DON'S WRISTWATCH. HE WAS WEARING IT WHEN HE... SAVED THOSE CHILDREN...
IT REMINDS US HOW BRAVE HE WAS...

FOUR-ELEVEN. THAT WOULD BE NINE-ELEVEN IN LONDON. BUT THAT WOULD MEAN I BECAME DOVE BEFORE DON DIED... NOT AFTER!
THEN THE VOICES DIDN'T GIVE ME THE POWER BECAUSE HE WAS DEAD...
THEY TOOK THE POWER FROM HIM.
THEY KILLED HIM LIKE...

...A MOUSE IN A MAZE...
HANK!

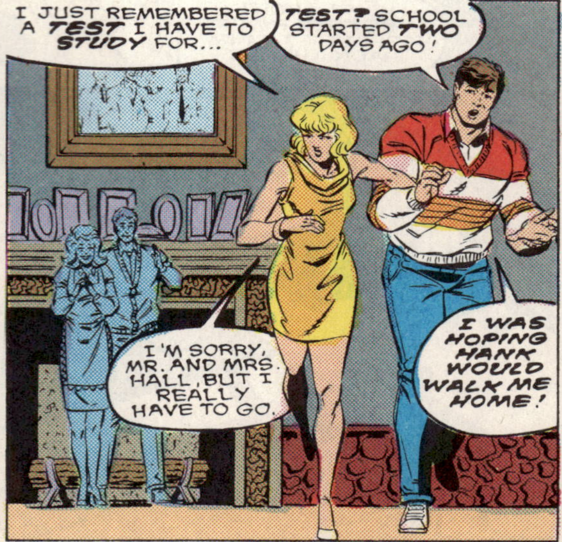
I JUST REMEMBERED A TEST I HAVE TO STUDY FOR...
TEST? SCHOOL STARTED TWO DAYS AGO!
I'M SORRY, MR. AND MRS. HALL, BUT I REALLY HAVE TO GO.
I WAS HOPING HANK WOULD WALK ME HOME!

WHAT WAS THAT ALL ABOUT?
HANK, KESTREL WAS RIGHT. WE DON'T KNOW ENOUGH ABOUT WHY WE'RE HAWK AND DOVE.
HE SAID WE'RE AN EXPERIMENT. WHAT DID HE MEAN?

ARE WE PART OF SOME PLAN CONCERNING ORDER AND CHAOS? IF SO, WHOSE PLAN? WHO WERE THOSE VOICES?
THERE'S SO MANY MISSING PIECES.
GIRL--YOU THINK TOO MUCH!
WE'RE HAWK AND DOVE 'CAUSE WE WERE IN THE RIGHT PLACE AT THE RIGHT TIME.

AND NOW WE CAN HELP PEOPLE... BASH GOONS... MAYBE EVEN SAVE THE WORLD ON A GOOD DAY.
WHAT MORE DO YOU NEED TO KNOW?

EVERYTHING.

LOOK--YOU DON'T HAVE TO PROVE YOURSELF TO ME.
I GAVE YOU A ROUGH TIME WHEN YOU FIRST SHOWED UP BECAUSE OF DON.
I REALLY LOVED THAT NUT.

I DIDN'T WANT TO BE REMINDED OF HIM, Y'KNOW.
BUT I DON'T WANT TO FORGET HIM.
I KEPT THINKING A NEW DOVE WOULD MAKE ME FORGET.

I WAS WRONG.
I THINK OF DON EVERY TIME YOU'RE DOVE. YOU DO HIM PROUD.
UH...NOT THAT YOU LOOK LIKE HIM, BUT...

LOOK, DAWN-- YOU'RE A SHARP GAL. REAL SMART WITH FINE LINES, AND I LIKE YOU, BUT I'M JUST NOT INTERESTED IN YOU THAT WAY...
I'LL GET OVER IT, HANK. HONEST.
YOU TWO SHOULD BE MORE CAREFUL...

HEY!
HI REN!
JUST SITTING HERE I HEARD EVERYTHING OF COURSE, I ALREADY KNEW THE HAWK AND DOVE PART, BUT WHAT IF I'D BEEN CAPTAIN BOOMERANG?
AREN'T YOU SUPER-TYPES SUSPICIOUS OF SHADOWY TYPES?
MAYBE YOU SHOULD REREAD THE MANUAL!

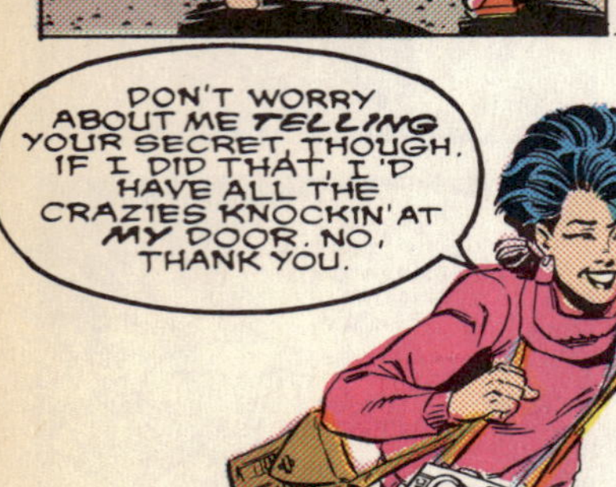
DON'T WORRY ABOUT ME TELLING YOUR SECRET, THOUGH. IF I DID THAT, I'D HAVE ALL THE CRAZIES KNOCKIN' AT MY DOOR. NO, THANK YOU.

OF COURSE, IT WOULD BE NICE IF MY DISCRETION WERE REWARDED WITH, SAY...

...A DATE WITH THE NEAREST BACHELOR... WHY, HERE'S ONE NOW! GEORGETOWN'S OWN HANK HALL!
WHO? ME?
UH...YEAH...I'D REALLY LIKE THAT, ACTUALLY...
GREAT! FRIDAY, EIGHT O'CLOCK. YOUR PLACE FOR SCARY MOVIES?

HELP, SOMEONE! HE'S GOT A KNIFE!
HANK, HE'S COMING THIS WAY. SHOULD WE--?
YEAH! 'SCUSE US, REN-- GOTTA GET TO WORK!
FRIDAY. JUST BE BACK BY THEN!

HAWK!
DOVE!
ROB
KARL
9.15.88

Other DC Universe collections available are:

TRADE PAPERBACKS

The Art of Walter Simonson

Batman: Blind Justice
Sam Hamm/Denys Cowan/Dick Giordano

Batman: The Collected Adventures Vol. 1
Kelley Puckett/Ty Templeton/Brad Rader/Rick Burchett

Batman: The Cult
Jim Starlin/Bernie Wrightson

Batman: The Dailies Vol.1 1943-44

Batman: The Dailies Vol.2 1944-45

Batman: The Dailies Vol.3 1945-46

Batman: The Dark Knight Returns
Frank Miller/Lynn Varley/Klaus Janson

Batman: Gothic
Grant Morrison/Klaus Janson

Batman: Prey
Doug Moench/Paul Gulacy/Terry Austin

Batman: Shaman
Dennis O'Neil/Edward Hannigan/John Beatty

Batman: The Sunday Classics 1943-46

Batman: Sword of Azrael
Dennis O'Neil/Joe Quesada/Kevin Nowlan

Batman: Tales of the Demon
Dennis O'Neil/Neal Adams/Dick Giordano, et al.

Batman: Venom
Dennis O'Neil/Trevor Von Eeden/Russell Braun/José Luis García-López

Batman: Year One
Frank Miller/David Mazzucchelli

Batman: Year Two
Mike Barr/Alan Davis/Todd McFarlane/Paul Neary/Alfredo Alcala

Batman vs. Predator: The Collected Edition
Dave Gibbons/Andy Kubert/Adam Kubert

Catwoman: Her Sister's Keeper
Mindy Newell/J.J. Birch/Michael Bair

Cosmic Odyssey
Jim Starlin/Mike Mignola/Carlos Garzon

Deathstroke, the Terminator: Full Cycle
Marv Wolfman/Steve Erwin/Will Blyberg

The Essential Showcase 1956-1959

The Greatest 1950s Stories Ever Told

The Greatest Batman Stories Ever Told Vol. 1

The Greatest Batman Stories Ever Told Vol. 2

The Greatest Flash Stories Ever Told

The Greatest Joker Stories Ever Told

The Greatest Superman Stories Ever Told

The Greatest Team-Up Stories Ever Told

Green Arrow: The Longbow Hunters
Mike Grell

Green Lantern/Green Arrow: Hard-Traveling Heroes
Dennis O'Neil/Neal Adams

Green Lantern/Green Arrow: More Hard-Traveling Heroes
Dennis O'Neil/Neal Adams/various

Hawkman
Gardner Fox/Joe Kubert

Hawkworld
Tim Truman/Alcatena

Justice League: A New Beginning
Keith Giffen/J.M. DeMatteis/Kevin Maguire

Justice League International: The Secret Gospel of Maxwell Lord
Keith Giffen/J.M. DeMatteis/Kevin Maguire/Al Gordon, et al.

Legion of Super-Heroes: The Great Darkness Saga
Paul Levitz/Keith Giffen/Larry Mahlstedt

Lobo's Greatest Hits

Lobo: The Last Czarnian
Keith Giffen/Alan Grant/Simon Bisley

Lobo's Back's Back
Keith Giffen/Alan Grant/Simon Bisley/Christian Alamy

The New Teen Titans: The Judas Contract
Marv Wolfman/George Pérez

The Spectre: Crimes and Punishments
John Ostrander/Tom Mandrake

World's Finest
Dave Gibbons/Steve Rude/Karl Kesel

STANDARD FORMAT BOOKS

Batman: A Death in the Family
Jim Starlin/Jim Aparo/Mike DeCarlo

Batman: A Lonely Place of Dying
Marv Wolfman/George Pérez/
Jim Aparo, et al.

Green Lantern: Emerald Dawn
Keith Giffen/Gerard Jones/Jim Owsley/
M.D. Bright/Romeo Tanghal

The Many Deaths of the Batman
John Byrne/Jim Aparo/Mike DeCarlo

Legends: The Collected Edition
John Ostrander/Len Wein/John Byrne/
Karl Kesel

The Man of Steel
John Byrne/Dick Giordano

Robin: A Hero Reborn
Chuck Dixon/Tom Lyle/Bob Smith

Robin: Tragedy and Triumph
Chuck Dixon/Alan Grant/Norm Breyfogle/
Tom Lyle/Steve Mitchell /Dick Giordano/
Bob Smith

Secret Origins of the World's Greatest Super-Heroes

Superman: Panic in the Sky
Various

Superman: The Death of Superman
Various

Superman: World Without a Superman
Various

HARDCOVER BOOKS

All Star Comics Archives Vol. 1

All Star Comics Archives Vol. 2

Batman Archives Vol. 1

Batman Archives Vol. 2

Batman Archives Vol. 3

Batman: The Dark Knight Archives Vol. 1

Green Lantern Archives

Justice League of America Archives Vol. 1

Justice League of America Archives Vol. 2

Legion of Super-Heroes Archives Vol. 1

Legion of Super-Heroes Archives Vol. 2

Legion of Super-Heroes Archives Vol. 3

SHAZAM! Archives Vol. 1

Superman Archives Vol. 1

Superman Archives Vol. 2

Superman Archives Vol. 3

The Greatest Golden Age Stories Ever Told

The Greatest Team-Up Stories Ever Told

COMING SOON

Legion of Super-Heroes Archives Vol. 4

Batman: Faces

Batman: The Collected Adventures Vol. 2